Praise for Tsipi Keller's Previous Novels

Praise for *Jackpot*

A Bahamian vacation turns into a nightmarish dreamworld in Tsipi Keller's smart, sly *Jackpot*. Maggie has long been cowed by her beautiful friend Robin, so when Robin leaves Paradise Island for a spur-of-the-moment sailing trip, Maggie has a chance to shine. Instead, she descends into wild gambling and even wilder sex, though she somehow retains her innocence. Keller expertly charts Maggie's transformation in this accomplished and oddly gripping novel. —**Publishers Weekly**

Keller, then, is bilingual when it comes to the discourse of emotion: she understands both the language of bland social accommodation and the language of excessive despair. The former shouts at us like an alibi, jarring in its cheerfulness. The latter is inarticulate and sulking and overcomes us in its morbid embrace. It's as if this book were written both by a Henry James and a Hubert Selby, Jr.: a glittering chronicler of social mores, where exterior and interior worlds interweave a rich tapestry, and a poète maudit, who savors the most abject and perverse treasures of the human condition.

—Bruce Benderson/The Brooklyn Rail

Tsipi Keller's *Jackpot* reminds me of Jean Rhys like no book I've read in years. I love Rhys; that's high praise. It's also a consumer warning: This book is a study in self-destruction. It's addictive, intense—a psychological page-turner that doesn't miss a beat. It's sexy as hell. But, for readers who like their fiction as crisply edged as their lawns, it's much too disturbing for the beach or daily commute… And when it's over? Maggie's in a zone you wouldn't have predicted. And so are you. Proof, I'd say, of an exceptional work of fiction.

—Jesse Kornbluth/HeadButler.com

This marvelously engaging and pleasurable novel is like a cross between watching a sly Eric Rohmer film about the spiritual crisis of vacation and reading a Jean Rhys interior monologue of a woman in extremis. For all its horrific aspects, it has a steady undercurrent of humor: the comedy derives from showing the precise mechanisms of low self-esteem, rationalization and self-indulgence. A wickedly readable, psychologically astute and drolly knowing fiction.　　**—Phillip Lopate**

The problem with novels of degradation is that the depressing nature of the narrative slows down the reading. If you like the character, then you'll not like seeing the character take a trip down the big swirly. Keller gets the reader past this with her present-tense prose and the wealth of understated humor inherent in her perspective on her character… The publisher of Keller's novel, Spuyten Duyvil, is not exactly a household name, but they have a huge line of original fiction available in these attractive trade paperback editions.　　**—Rick Kleffel/Agony Column**

The original literary characters to be obsessed by what proved to be a false paradise from which they felt excluded, and who found what they thought was a neat short-cut which ended up taking them in the opposite direction, were Milton's Adam and Eve. The imaginative brilliance of *Jackpot* is reflected in its ability to reveal and make new this archetypal pattern, while seeming to focus so relentlessly and exclusively on the here and now immediacy of Maggie and her small world. This is an extraordinary achievement, made even more so by the extent to which it seems hidden, at first, within the fabric of the book's compelling realism and accessibility.　　**—Andrew Kaufman**

It isn't very long before you realize that Keller has caught you in a deceptive web of shallow ideals and insanity that in no way resemble the bland Ally McBeal psycho-babble you were prepared for. As a matter of fact it's closer to the ever-descending rings of hell of Hubert Selby's

Requiem for a Dream. Unlike the intensity of Selby's work, Keller's story has a hypnotic, seductive quality that pulls the reader further into Maggie's escalating disintegration.

—Paul McDonald/Louisville Courier Journal

I guess you could call *Jackpot* a beach read's worst nightmare, in the best possible sense: sun, sand, and palm trees cannot begin to mask the dark corners of this paradise. **—Robert Gray/Fresh Eyes**

Tsipi Keller's new novel *Jackpot* is a skillfully plotted story of a character's unraveling, so gradual and inexorable that you move from comfort level to comfort level without realizing how uncomfortable you're getting, like the proverbial frog in the pot… One thinks, oddly enough, of *The House of Mirth.* Though Maggie doesn't have to fall as far as Lily Bart, she falls in the same curious stepwise fashion… One thinks, too—continuing the theme of the American fallen-woman novel—of *The Awakening*, but *Jackpot* is very much a postmodern fallen-woman novel, without any of the moral and social anxieties that characterize even as modernist a work *as The Awakening.* **—Tim Morris/Lection**

Jackpot is a wonder of a book. It is irresistibly fascinating—painfully fascinating. You may not feel like sharing the experiences of its misguided heroine, but you should, because you'll have a livelier time sticking with her than to your own comfortable ways. And you can always reassure yourself that you'll never end up like Maggie; although—who knows?—some day you may get the chance. **—Harry Mathews**

Praise for *Retelling*

The mystery of who butchered ethereally beautiful and pregnant Elsbeth is at the heart of Keller's elegant and spooky second novel (part of a trilogy, after *Jackpot*). Was it the traumatized and fragile narrator,

Sally, whose friendship with the dead woman verged on the obsessive? Or was it Elsbeth's arrogant and demanding boyfriend, Drew, who resented Sally's relationship with her? Keller flirts with the answer as her novel slips back and forth through time to depict tantalizing glimpses of possible truths filtered through Sally's uncertain memories. The police, bent on extracting a confession from Sally, harangue her during increasingly abusive interrogation sessions that provide her a forum for creepily pondering her (questionable) innocence. This opaque yet beguiling novel showcases the work of a talented and original writer.

—**Publishers Weekly**

Readers of Dostoyevsky's *Crime and Punishment* always know that Raskolnikov committed murder, but they often don't know whether Raskolnikov knows that he committed murder... In her new trilogy, Tsipi Keller is revealed as a superlative psychological novelist: "It was the end of the millennium, life rushed at me, the streets reeked of urine. Everybody talked but nobody listened. Men in suits shook hands as if important matters were at stake. It was all a game."

—**Joshua Cohen/The Forward**

All of this gives the impression that Sally isn't someone you'd want to invite over for a nightcap—not without hiding the knives first. But *Retelling* is great at maintaining mind-bending suspense, and it never entirely rules out the possibility that its narrator is simply an odd case. The book questions its own sense of reality a few times too many, but the buildup is justified by the powerful final arc. In the end, Keller gives her narrator's eerie delusions free reign—an apt conclusion for this heartfelt and willfully perverse novel.

—**Michael Miller/TimeOut**

What do you get when you mix a Rashomon narrative with a Hitchcockian detective esthetic? You get *Retelling*, by Tsipi Keller. Not

only that, you get an us against them scenario that constricts tighter as it seemingly unfolds letting you know the universe has other plans beyond comprehension and to attempt understanding is to deal in frustration...
In conclusion, we come away with a rich and tightly woven suspense story from Tsipi Keller, a master storyteller of the modern world, who assembles her palette of color and texture in the most exquisitely sensual ways... Not afraid to wear her influences on her sleeve, she does so humbly and without guile, as she offers her predecessors a grand and glorious complement by way of her deft display of mastery under their auspices.
—C.B Smith/MadHatterReview

As in Keller's previous book, *Jackpot* (both novels are part of a planned trilogy), *Retelling* foregrounds a meek, solitary woman (the late Elsbeth once mocked Sally as "the little mouse, nibbling on books in the dark") who's bereft when her imperious pal disappears, leaving the beta-girl without a light source to illuminate her own half-formed personality... Capturing the waft and drift of her un-heroine's unstructured days, Keller has a keen eye for the territorial pissings and unspoken resentments of immature female friendships.
—Jessica Winter/The Village Voice

Praise for *Elsa*

Elsa is the third in Tsipi Keller's trilogy of psychological novels. The first two were *Jackpot* and *Retelling*, which trace the fortunes of women. *Elsa* calls to mind some of Richard Burgin's noir fiction. Both writers explore the world of nefarious, but initially engaging, operators who insinuate themselves into the lives of lonely strangers aiming to control or ruin them.... Much more than a tale about a smart woman who makes foolish choices, *Elsa* is a fast-paced, tightly crafted, suspenseful, psychological crime novel that sidles up to the reader, then pounces.
—Lynn Levin/Cleaver Magazine

Elsa is a woman of thirty-nine: a tax lawyer who lives alone with her cat. She talks about men with her friends. She is a classic literary figure, a Madame Bovary in the twenty-first century. Tsipi Keller is more than aware of this, as Flaubert sticks his head in at one point: "The promise of love, faint as it is, does wonders for her. The promise of love, of romance, of beautiful sex. So what if women, to believe Flaubert, mistake their vaginas for their hearts? So what? Let them. Let her. What does Flaubert know about love? Let her mistake what part she chooses for her heart." —**Evan Steuber/American Book Review**

Praise for *The Prophet of Tenth Street*

Tsipi Keller has taken us into a writer's very being…. This is a provocative story that stays with the reader. —**Jewish Book World**

Poet and novelist Keller (*Retelling*) handles this poignant tale with the deftness of a writer who has struggled alongside her characters.
—**Publishers Weekly**

It is beyond difficult to write fiction about a fiction-maker; not only do you have to get into the guy's head, you've got to create a plot in which something actually happens. Keller does both, and in a way that's unnerving--how does she know so much about what it means to be a man, trapped in his head, convinced he will find and reveal the essential truths of life? —**Head Butler**

nadja

on

nadja

TSIPI KELLER

UNDERGROUND VOICES

Published by Underground Voices
www.undergroundvoices.com
Editor contact: Cetywa Powell

Library of Congress Cataloging-in-Publication Data:
Keller, Tsipi.
Nadja on Nadja (paperback)
2018954831

ISBN #: 978-0-9988923-5-1
Printed in the United States of America.

The quote that ends the book is from *The Dwarf* by Pär Lagerkvist, translated from the Swedish by Alexandra Dick (Sibyl Alexandra Erikson, 1906-1989), Hill and Wang, Inc. 1945

Excerpts from the novel have appeared, in modified form, in *Blunderbuss* (2016, "Nadja on Nadja"), and in *Vestiges 03: Mimesis* (2017, "Dots on the Horizon")

"I would like my pictures to look as if a human being had passed between them, like a snail, leaving a trail of the human presence, memory trace of past events, as the snail leaves its slime."

—Francis Bacon

"Feminine Psychology: It is said that the turtledove never drinks clear water, but always muddies it first with its foot so that it may the better suit its pensive mind."

Journals/Katherine Mansfield

More often than not, Nadja likes to spend time in her head, a place she knows well and feels comfortable in. Right now she is at work, walking down the corridor toward a corporeal place of promise where she will steal a few moments and take what she calls a Breathing Break. The best place for a BB is the bathroom. The bathroom may not be very appealing, but it is roomy, usually free of unpleasant odors and, most importantly, usually empty. At the far end, there is a large window and that is where she is headed, having made sure that all five stalls are vacant. She plants her right foot on the ledge and, leaning elbow on thigh, she observes the street from her twelfth floor perch.

Yes, she is the small animal in the confines of its cage, albeit with certain workplace amenities, such as WC facilities and free-roaming ruminations. Looking down on the street and listening in on her thoughts, it occurs to her that she could jump. She imagines the fear catching in her throat as the wind rushes past her face—the sheer, if brief, exhilaration of giving in to nihilism and madness. In another part of her brain, it surprises her that she, of all people, would even entertain such a thought; she who, in spite of everything, is usually optimistic, not to say hopeful, and is always aware of what is good and what is bad for her.

In the building across the street, people stoop over desks or stare at screens, and she feels for them; like her, they may be thinking: It's so beautiful out, and we are stuck indoors.

Her particular indoors is the research library of a large accounting firm. A library of few real books, it consists mostly of computers. There are people, too, whose job it is to punch in and to retrieve data for the accountants, as well as documents for the legal department. Down below is the glamour of Fifth Avenue, the business and tourist center of the new world. Men in suits, women in dresses, preoccupied and fiercely adhering to the future at hand, march onward fast in slow motion. A friendly sun beats down on their heads. Humanity, as if spellbound, is approaching the end of the millennium.

When in a certain mood, like now, kind of downcast but not severely so, Nadja, wittingly or unwittingly, goes back and reexamines the bad moments in her life, not bad-bad but kind of humiliating, kind of still wounding and perplexing when she revisits them, like the time she went away for the weekend with a new lover, or someone she thought would become a lover, even though he was older than her by at least ten years, already divorced and with young kids the wife got to keep. At one point during the weekend, she left her flimsy—she did not think it flimsy at the time, but she was young and inexperienced then—black slip on the bed, which, she reddens again at the thought, must have been some type of synthetic fabric. The prospective lover had just come out of the bathroom and, approaching the bed, he picked up the slip with two fingers, took a look at it, and let it drop. Not a word was exchanged, it lasted no longer than a second, and she, well, she instantly caught, or intuited, the whiff emanating from him, the whiff of contempt, maybe mild and bemused, but contempt nonetheless, not so much contempt for her, as an all-encompassing contempt for cheap.

The moment came and went, and she soon forgot about it, they had a nice weekend together, nice for her at least, he treated her well, took her to expensive restaurants she was unaccustomed to, but later, in bed, she apparently failed him again, and he apologized, saying he could not get hard for her. He was gentle when he said it, his voice soft and regretful, assuring her it was not her fault, it was his, hinting that he favored naughty and lewd. Still, during the weeks and years that followed, the slip had crystallized in her mind and gradually became the symbol of her inadequacy, socially and otherwise: she was not up to standard. She would never be up to standard in anything she undertook.

Indeed, most mornings she wakes with a heart that still beats, but is heavy with defeatist thoughts about the futility of life, *her* life, and, reluctant to face the day she burrows deeper into the covers, seeking shelter in darkness. Unhelpfully, she remembers that she is alone in the world, and not as smart and "with it" as others seem to be, and that her only true talents are hope and delusion. But, she reminds herself, she does have a gift: she is tenacious. And being tenacious means she wants to live. Wanting to live means she must compete, she must participate. She tells herself that these bad, early-morning thoughts are just the residue of some dream she dreamt in the night, and that the sooner she is up and running, the better; and soon she does, she jumps out of bed with sudden determination, and the mere physicality of movement alters something in her brain, and she is awake and back in the column of the living.

Jolted out of her reveries at the sound of marching high heels in the corridor, Nadja quickly shuts herself in the nearest stall. Over the years, she has managed to establish a proper, if distant, relationship with her co-workers; they know enough to leave her alone. She is dimly aware that they think she is odd, and her frequent visits to the bathroom, no doubt, are a topic of conversation. She did tell them once that she has back problems and that she comes in here to do her yoga stretches. Not that they ever saw her do any yoga. Maybe they believe her back problems story, or maybe they think she suffers from some urinary disorder. It is also true that, in the office, she needs to pee more often, a condition she accredits to working with Jerry.

This time it is Colleen invading the quiet of her sanctum. Colleen has been sent on a mission, which she cheerfully executes. She bursts into the bathroom, calling, "Nadja, Jerry wants you."

Jerry. The Boss. Long tentacles. He always finds her. Like an ardent devotee, he needs her at his side, ever so silent and subdued.

For a brief moment, Nadja shuts her eyes, then speaks. "What's the urgency, Colleen? Tell him I'm otherwise engaged."

Colleen's laugh rings out, and Nadja imagines her primping in front of the mirror: a tall, big-boned girl of thirty. Oblivious and healthy-looking in her good skin, her thick chestnut hair, her green eyes. Colleen is engaged to be married to boyfriend Robert. Colleen, Nadja reflects, is everything that Nadja is not.

"What can I tell you, Nadja? Finish up."

The door slams and Nadja comes out of the stall. She walks to the sink and slowly washes her hands, if only to approximate the real time in case Jerry has his finger on his stopwatch. She is a slave and, barring a miracle, will probably remain one for a long time. On the whole, Nadja consoles herself, things are not all that bad. As much as she hates the office and feels she is being exploited, at the very least she manages to exploit them back, appropriating precious time to do her own work. True, conditions are not optimal, she is not allowed the silent, grass-growing mood Melville talked about, Melville who slaved as a Customs Inspector in New York.

And her paycheck, too, is not to be sneered at. A paycheck, a checkbook, is a wonderful thing. When she sits down to pay her bills, when she signs checks, she fancies herself an active member of society. During moments of grace, she likes to imagine that the other elves in the office, as they huddle in their cubicles, are also engaged in illicit work, and that Jerry himself is working on a book, possibly a memoir. It is an interesting possibility, and maybe a good idea for a story, the idea that they are all complicit partners in a system that has warped them. At the same time, she also worries that working on the sly adversely affects her brain, as well as her budding novel. It burns a hole in her, the fact that she has to do her work stealthily as if it were a shameful act.

But, not to forget: there's the weekend to look forward to. Tomorrow night, for a change, Raoul is staying over, and Friday morning they will drive out to Long Island to visit Sabine; like any normal couple, they have plans for the weekend. All she need do is erect a bridge over the gap between now and tomorrow evening and make Jerry disappear under. Jerry, the Library Director, lording over a few female elves who have become expert at filling requests and staying out of trouble.

Nadja wipes her hands and leans closer to the mirror. What a face! She used to delight in her face and easily match its reflection with a purity she felt inside, but lately, and even longer than lately, she has not been able to match the inside with the outside; something has gone missing. Or, conversely, something has been added, something intangible, and yet as real as time. The purity is still there, she hopes, but the reflection has been changing on her in small subtle ways that make her look severe, or tired. People around her may not notice these minute changes, but she does. Very possibly because her eyes are actively searching for signs that she is no longer the carefree girl that used to reside in her. If this is so, she'd better stop looking at herself.

Looking at herself, Nadja lets out a sigh. Jerry is waiting—she can almost hear the tap-tap of his fingers on his desk. But she likes it in here, AND, she is taking a break in the only private room on the floor. This is where she hides when she needs to recharge whatever needs recharging in order to endure the hours ahead. True, she spends a good chunk of her day working on Woman Ending Badly; still, it takes a lot out of her, not so much the writing as having to be on the lookout for Jerry who may suddenly materialize at her desk to check up on her. Jerry who gets lonely and restless, sitting all alone with his power, and, every so often, emerges from his office to survey the minions of his kingdom.

Nadja blinks a few times, and attempts a smile at her reflection. Okay, maybe it is not her face that is the problem. Maybe her eyes are to blame, they mislead her. They are two dark dots staring back at her, and, when tired, they prejudice the way she sees the world, including her own face. Still, when she thinks that she looks awful, she instinctively accepts the judgment and is bound to make decisions. She will stop smoking. She will drop Raoul and find a new lover. She will quit her job, she will not touch desserts, she will cut down on wine. She will drink more water, will make time for exercise, and will concentrate on breathing correctly. It is one thing to complain about your looks, another, to do something about it, short of going to a specialist and paying him to fix it.

adja walks into Jerry's office—a neat, medium-size box with a medium-size window. Upon seeing her, Jerry tightens his lips and lays his hands on the desk, as if to anchor himself.

"Nadja," he says, choking on her name. "Why do you disappear on me all the time?"

Indeed, why? Imperceptibly, Nadja raises her heels a couple of inches off the floor, and then eases herself down, working her calf muscles. She is thinking of Betty, Jerry's secretary, who told her in confidence that Jerry's wife, a beautician, dyes his hair and mustache. The wife also manicures his nails, and Nadja imagines the two of them, husband and wife, bound together over his fingernails, in their innocent, yet crafty, endeavor to boost the breadwinner's image. Maybe this is what brings them close, a couple in cahoots against the rest of the world.

"I was in the kitchen," Nadja says, subliminally suggesting to Jerry that the kitchen is where she and all females belong, in his mind at least. Yet Jerry does not seem to appreciate her attempt at humor; she cannot charm the man. He eyes her, not inviting her to sit, which is both a good and a bad sign: he will not keep her long; but he is obviously in one of his "moods." They say men do not have periods or PMS issues, but sometimes she really wonders.

"You know," Jerry says, "it is such a mystery to me and, need I add, to many others in the office, how a woman like you, a woman in your position, does not even realize…" He finds her so unworthy of attention, he does not bother to complete the sentence. He sits on his throne, a prince, unaware that, like any mortal, his days are numbered. The window is at his back, and it happens sometimes during a meeting that Nadja idly watches as the man and his chair catapult through glass and steel out the window. Jerry is in his fifties and, like most short men, walks like a peacock, his head held high, sporting reddish curly hair and a reddish mustache. One morning, he passed Nadja on the street on the way to the office. He did not see her, but she noticed him right away because of his impossibly rigid posture. His ears were plugged, and he walked past her, a beatific expression on his face, and Nadja wondered what he was listening to.

"Phil tells me"—Jerry leans forward in his chair—"that you're procrastinating. He doesn't get from you the cooperation he requires on the Information Project."

The Information Project is Jerry's pet, an on-going project that she and Phil have been working on for the last few months. Every Thursday, at eleven, they go into Jerry's office, presumably to report on their progress, but in fact to make Jerry feel important and "on top of things."

"I'm not procrastinating," Nadja says. She considers pointing out that Phil can hardly get any work done if he sits all day in Jerry's office, keeping him company. Instead, she concentrates on Jerry's short, stunted fingers, on the painfully dry skin that reminds her of dead baby lizards.

"I see," Jerry says. With surprising dexterity, his fingers come to life on the desk, as if striking a keyboard. "So Phil is lying, and you are working as hard as you know how."

"I do," she replies in the same tone as his: cold and matter-of-fact.

"Don't get smart with me, Nadja." Blood is draining from his face and Nadja holds her breath. Maybe blood is draining from her face as well. In sympathy. She doesn't hate him so much as she hates herself in his company. "Whatever happened to the Efficiency Report?"

"I'm working on it. I'll have it for you in a few days."

"You're working on it." Jerry looks up at her. His blue eyes are bloodshot, and Nadja wonders if Jerry and his wife lead a wild sex life. Like Sabine says, it is the ordinary folk who go for the strange and kinky. Jerry is slim, but the wife is heavy; Nadja saw her once when she appeared in the office, assuming the same haughty and proprietary mien as her husband. Nadja sometimes indulges in imagining little Jerry buried under his wife, suffocating under the weight of the massive, cellulite-wrinkled thighs, the pendulous, maternal breasts. Sometimes she tries to imagine him atop the wife, but the image is too grotesque.

"Need I remind you," Jerry changes his tone. "You're two weeks past your deadline."

"I should be done early next week, it's very near completion," she says earnestly. It is creepy, she reflects, how she can have all kinds of thoughts about Jerry while looking straight at him, innocent-like. It is even creepier to contemplate that while she is having her thoughts about him, Jerry is having his thoughts about her.

"I have to tell you, Nadja," Jerry says gravely, "I won't tolerate the situation much longer."

He seems to draw pleasure from the gravity of his words, and for a moment she stands there, unsure how to respond. In all the years they have been working together, he has never threatened her.

"What do you mean?" she asks, truly baffled. Often she will say, "What do you mean?" knowing full well what he means.

"Your behavior, especially lately, is increasingly more disagreeable, and certainly too erratic for a corporate setting."

With an impatient flutter of his hand, Jerry dismisses her, and she checks an urge to offer her rendition of a military salute. The fact of the matter is: the Efficiency Report has been ready for a while, but it is a rule with her: delay submission until the very last moment so he does not dump new assignments on her head. Her behavior, he says, is too erratic for a corporate setting. He may have a point there—Nadja experiences a flicker of remorse. Maybe Jerry is a nice man, and she, a tormentor against her will, brings out the worst in him.

At the next desk, Colleen is laughing her loud laugh. Colleen can do whatever she wants and no one will complain. She is a jolly, loyal worker, always patient and willing to help. She comes to work with the attitude: I am here for eight hours, I will do whatever they want me to do: my time is theirs. Body and soul, she belongs to the office, to the corporation. She is also the official disseminator of gossip and news. At times, for short spells, Nadja wishes she had Colleen's bouncy disposition.

"Want to hear a funny story?" Colleen calls to her.

"Not right now, Colleen, I need to take care of something."

"Gosh, you're so busy all the time."

Nadja inserts her USB drive in the port under the desk and soon her manuscript appears on the screen. She is up to page thirty-four, and there is yet a long way to go, and many important decisions are yet to be made. Nadja feels a peculiar, stirring affection for Woman, so tall and elegant on her high heels, now marching into the office of this senior partner, a man she dreads. Every time she is alone with him, it feels as though he is doing something he should not be doing, and Woman keeps her eyes on his face as if unaware of his hand disappearing under the desk, as if unaware of the way he suddenly hoists himself and pulls at his crotch. Are his pants too tight, or is he trying to cue her? she wonders, all the while pretending not to notice, but of course she does notice, how could she not, while also asking herself how long will she be able to endure the tension, this pantomimed power play, before she bursts and breaks into tiny little pieces right before his eyes. Does his behavior qualify as sexual harassment? What would she say in court? He played with his balls?

Later, on the steps of St. Patrick's Cathedral, Nadja is spooning her lunch: frozen yogurt in a plastic container to be rinsed and recycled: quick and efficient, the tenets of modern city life. She is part of a great human mass, sprawled on the steps—a sea of personalities, not an inch to be spared. For a moment, she becomes acutely aware of her neighbors' physical presence, and is glad to be sitting there, among them. They are all breathing, wanting, hurting creatures. Tonight, tomorrow, one of them may be dead.

Nadja shuts her eyes, abandons herself to sunshine and the illusion of freedom. She wonders how the tradition began, who was the first person to take lunch on the steps, and others followed. We are solitary beings, she muses, and yet we like the company of others. In the city, at least. Taking lunch in the woods, she would resent the stranger who may suddenly appear, picking her small corner of paradise. All would be ruined: her fantasy, her appetite, her love for nature and living things.

One o'clock. She must rise and leave behind this vibrant urban landscape; a lethargic afternoon, on a low-ceilinged, colorless floor, awaits her. A floor subdivided into sections and cubicles, occupied by humans hunched over uniformly standard office desks. Already, walking back to the office, she wishes she could lie down somewhere and take a nap.

Upstairs, clocks are ticking: on walls, on phones, on screens, but not fast enough. Woman is still in a meeting with the senior partner. As she concentrates on his face, Woman worries that she may be concentrating too hard, unwittingly revealing her anxiety; her face, she knows, is an open book. Maybe she is imagining the whole thing, maybe his thoughts are clean. Maybe he is just moving his hand up and down his thigh. It could be a nervous tic. Maybe he has sweaty hands. Maybe he is emotionally unbalanced and moving his hand up and down his thigh comforts him.

Suddenly inspired, Nadja reaches for the phone and dials Raoul's number. She hopes to get him on the line rather than his secretary, a middle-aged woman who guards her boss with jealous devotion. The way she announces, "Mr. Bauer's office," makes Nadja feel that even his secretary has a right to him more than she does.

"This is Nadja. May I speak to him, please?"

There is a pause, fraught with righteous indignation. "Just a moment," the secretary says and transfers the call.

"I can't talk now, Nadja, I'm going into a meeting."

"Wait, I must ask you something. What does it feel like when you get an erection?"

"Where are you?"

"Where do you think? At work."

"What does it feel like?" Raoul sounds flustered.

"Yes, what does it feel like?"

"Well, it feels swollen, big and swollen."

"What do you mean big? Do small guys also feel big?"

"Nadja, I have to go into a meeting…" As Raoul says this, Nadja is prepared to laugh, thinking he's about to say, "…and I'm getting an erection." But Raoul says, "I'll think about it and call you later."

"No, now," she says. "I need to know now, it's important, just tell me quickly."

"I only have a minute." Raoul relents. "Well, there's this tingling sensation—"

"Really? Is it pleasant?"

"Oh yes, very. Arousal, you know. Women feel the same thing, I'm sure, only ours hangs out."

"Yours hangs out?" Nadja repeats, stalling for time. She does not like it when Raoul places himself, ever so innocently, in another camp, the camp of men; invariably, he sounds smug, superior.

Raoul laughs. "Well yes, you know."

"Do you feel your skin stretch?"

"I don't think so. It begins to grow and you feel these electric currents running up and down your body, ending in you balls, your entire crotch area. I imagine it must be different for non-circumcised men. For them the head probably wants to pop out. My head is already exposed…."

They are mirthful. Like two accomplices, they giggle into the phone. Possibly because they visualize the swollen head, or maybe because they are suddenly aware that they are discussing penises in the middle of the workday, while important men are waiting to start a meeting.

"Is it phone sex you want?"

"Wait. Do small guys also feel big when erect?"

"I don't know. I don't see why not. When it gets big, you want to touch it, or rub it against something, a woman, anything. That's part of what it is. It needs a rubbing, a stroking. Let me close the door here."

Again they laugh. Nadja is happy to hear herself laugh. She glances at Jerry's door, expecting him to emerge.

"Do you have an erection now?" she asks.

"No, just a mushroom."

"Portobello?"

"Oh, another thing. Your balls get bigger and very sensitive. Have I been helpful? May I begin my meeting?"

"Sure, go whip 'em."

I n her kitchen, Nadja tells herself she enjoys the quiet, the peace, and she does, yet Jerry is still with her. It upsets her that she brings him home with her. The guy has insinuated himself into her psyche, he has become an obsession. Nadja wonders if she is an obsession for him, if he thinks about her while in the bosom of his family, if he discusses her at the dinner table, talking about the insurgent he must send away in order to regain his peace of mind and fully enjoy his position in life. He has worked hard to get to where he is, and now, at the zenith of his career, why must he put up with a poorly dressed joy-killer like Nadja who mars his days at the office? He complains to the wife, and she, what else can she do but voice her support? "Get rid of this nuisance," she tells Jerry, just as Zeresh does in the Book of Esther, advising her husband Haman to hang Mordecai from the tallest tree. Mordecai, the Jew, and the only man at the palace gate who would not bow down before Haman, the king's right-hand man.

It is her own pride, Nadja concludes, that gets her in trouble; her pride, and her sense of fairness and justice, prod her to prove to Jerry that she is her own autonomous person. What a useless effort. Why can't she be normal and kiss his ass like she is supposed to? All it will take is a couple of minutes a day, running into his office to confer, to ask for his professional opinion, and even inquire about the wife and kids. That's all he wants from her, why can't she do it? Show a little deference even if she feels none? If she were smart in the ways that Phil is, she would be promoted, she would make more money, and still be able to work on Woman—in peace. It is rumored that Phil does some work for his wife on his computer, but no one bothers or spies on him. And Jerry has Betty do personal things for him, like paying his bills. She even types Jerry's daughter's school papers.

After two glasses of wine, it is easier for her to relax and divert her mind away from the office and from Jerry. She lies on the couch and watches a Nature documentary about frogs and snails. The frog takes a snail in its mouth and presently spits it out because the snail excretes some foul-tasting substance. The snail survives the experience, but the frog does not learn its lesson; it goes after another snail, and again spits it out. When she and Raoul eat escargot, the foul-tasting excretion, she supposes, has been dealt with somehow, unless what is foul-tasting to the frog is delicious to humans, what with all the butter and garlic.

In bed, Nadja reclines against the pillows with Beckett's *More Pricks than Kicks*. She reads for a while and then shifts her gaze to the dark window. Tomorrow night, Raoul will stay over and the weekend will begin for them. She looks forward to the weekend, to getting out of the city, and yet a vague anxiety agitates in her chest. Hoping to relieve it, Nadja devotes a moment to pleasant daydreaming: her work is published to wide acclaim, there is money in her bank account, she never has to go to the office again. Ah, what relief. She pulls a pillow to her and rubs her nose and lips against it; the fabric, cotton, is not the finest, it is a bit grainy, and yet it affords immediate contact and texture. She feels a pure, sudden joy at the physicality of things, and a soothing lull washes away her anxiety. Nadja is surprised and grateful for it; she did not expect such instantaneous calm.

They are both mildly high, heading east on the Long Island Expressway. Nadja, in the passenger seat, sits cross-legged. She is peeling half a stick of gum she will put in her mouth to fill it with flavor, at which time she will light a cigarette and take a couple of puffs. She measures everything, knows the exact small quantities she requires for momentary gratification. At the wheel is Raoul, a competent driver, lover, and part-time protector. He has both hands on the wheel, his entire being focused on the road. He is a man who takes his driving seriously, which may annoy her, depending on her mood. This morning she is inclined to be annoyed, even though she would much prefer it if she were in a better mood. Outside, it is a hot August morning; inside, it is a cool, enclosed universe. They had smoked half a joint before leaving her apartment, and Nadja entertains the thought that, glimpsed from outside, she and Raoul may resemble those stiff, shrouded dummies they use in the industry to test-crash a car.

"Let me have a shnickle," Raoul says, a shnickle being their pet word for "puff." But, he is too late. She has just killed the cigarette with her usual swiftness, expertly severing the burning tip, then puffing out the smoke still remaining in the body of her Marlboro.

"You always do that," Raoul states a fact in a resigned, slightly discontented voice; he is grumpy, too. The problem is, he takes his cues from her, even though she has told him a thousand times that when she is in a foul mood, she needs him to cheer her up.

"You're always a millisecond late," she says, trying not to sound gleeful. Indeed, she is glad that he is late: she keeps count of the cigarettes she smokes, and the less puffs he takes—Raoul is not a smoker—the more accurate the count. "I'll light it again in a little while."

But Raoul's discontent is still simmering. "They say it's not good for you to do that. You only inhale more germs or something."

"That's nonsense generated and propagated by the tobacco companies," she counters.

There is a short pause. "I love it." Raoul says, now letting his discontent break free, "when you think you know best."

Nadja turns to him. This man is her lover. Comfortably bourgeois, although he claims he wants more out of his life, and therefore sticks with her. She is an important part of his life, he whispers in her ear every so often, usually after sex, and she lies there thinking that Raoul is part of her life, too, but which part exactly? And what is her life, anyway? The more she thinks about it, the clearer it becomes that when she says "my life" she says something that makes sense but is meaningless. As long as she does not dwell on it, she can go on living her life. But as soon as she attempts to dive deeper and ponder such issues, a feeling of queasiness spreads in her stomach and a strange foggy somberness descends as if she has ventured too far and briefly touched something that is beyond her reach—perhaps forbidden, perhaps dangerous, perhaps an area in her brain where old phobias and superstitions lie in wait.

She cannot look at Raoul for long when he is not looking

at her. Maybe because it allows her to look at him with cold, judging eyes. Maybe because his profile seems alien, remote: all she sees are his nose and chin, not his best features. His hands, she thinks, grip the wheel too tightly. She wishes her lover had a more relaxed, cavalier attitude when it comes to driving, but this is a new car, and Raoul has been very fastidious about it. Abnormally so, she thinks. In fact, she resents the new car.

When she thinks such thoughts, cold and uncaring and critical of him, she reminds herself that he loves her, almost unconditionally. She misses the days when Raoul obeyed all her commands, worshipped her in fact. From the beginning, what moved and impressed her was the way he admired her—so openly, and without reserve. He still does, he is still wary of her, but dares to contradict her once in a while.

She says, "You get very contentious when you're high."

"I'm not high. You're the one who's high."

A bubble of hysterical laughter begins to rise in her. How absurd he is. Maybe they are both absurd. Together. She could easily turn this small outburst of his into an argument, but does she want to?

"All right, you're not high, but you're contentious."

"I don't like it when you dismiss what I say."

"What did you say?"

"Never mind."

Just like a married couple. She puts her hands in her lap and looks straight ahead. Her so-called life is in a state of flux. She feels there is something in the offing, that there is something she must do, but she is not yet sure what it is exactly, or what decision or direction she must take. The thought nags at her that she nags at him because she is unhappy. Is he the source of her unhappiness? Maybe, but her job takes first place. If she did not have Raoul, she would have no one—no lover, and no sex, of course. Chances are she would be even more miserable than she is now. Or maybe not. Maybe it would be good for her to be alone for a while. Maybe she needs someone new in her life.

Her thoughts are no help, they only bring more confusion. The trouble is: she will never know if Raoul admires her because she is admirable, or because he is married and is grateful to have her. It saddens her to consider that she and Raoul were meant for one another, perhaps for life, but circumstances will not allow them to fully explore the possibility. They both feel uncomfortable in the "situation." They tell each other they did not mean to fall in love, it was meant to be a short affair. They say it, but Nadja suspects they both know they are lying. She was looking to fall in love, not necessarily with Raoul, but with someone, and Raoul, so she believes, was looking for the same thing, to be in love again, not necessarily with her, but with someone.

"What are you thinking about?" Raoul asks.

"Are you sure we didn't miss the exit? It feels like we've been driving forever."

"That's why they call it Long Island," Raoul says in his exaggerated heavy accent.

Nadja laughs. It has never occurred to her to wonder why the island is called Long Island, and she appreciates this unexpected illumination of the name. She and Raoul do not get to spend many weekends together, why be morose when she can be happy? Her life is not all that bad. She is not a total failure, she does accomplish things, even if it takes her a little longer.

Encouraged, Raoul continues. "It should be renamed: Long Long Island."

Nadja laughs some more, biting into time.

Now it is her turn. "Very Long Long Island."

They laugh, they are happy, nearly restored to normalcy. Last night, they went out to eat, and Nadja, already satiated with good food and pleasure, looked at her favorite dessert— chocolate soufflé—which had just been placed before her. She picked up her spoon and punctured the top, admiring the dark liquid inside the crater.

"What do you see?" Raoul whispered at her side.

"I see," Nadja whispered back. "I see molten lava and I'm floating on it."

"Is it hot?"

"Oh yes, very, and velvety and rich."

"Is there room for me?"

Nadja, surprised, looked up at Raoul; a peculiar wistful expression sat on his face. "Always," she said, meaning it.

They were quite pleased, they were having a good night, which is not always the case. At times, they have a fight in the restaurant, not a loud fight, but a war of hardened eyes and tight lips.

Feeling somewhat better, she looks out the window, seemingly aloof behind her cool, dark shades, but actually checking out the passengers in passing cars, judging and comparing them with herself and Raoul. Most of the cars have the same compact, shiny look as theirs; they are the new middle class, heading for the shore, going 65-70 efficient mph. A huge truck looms in the right lane, dwarfing them. Nadja looks up, scrutinizes the strong, virile driver in the high cabin. She could have been with him, living a different life, driving cross-country, mile after mile of blissful insouciance, her hand on his thigh, his on hers. Occasionally they stop for fast food and sex.

For a stretch, the truck is parallel with their car. Mustache and sunglasses look down from the cabin and scrutinize her. Man to woman, woman to man; Raoul accelerates.

Ah, she sighs, the life of the mind, a short-lived fantasy. Idly she wonders if others indulge as promiscuously and deliberately as she in this futile mental exercise. Often, when she is in the grip of some elaborate dream-world, the pleasure is acutely physical (sexual fantasy) or acutely mental (a literary breakthrough).

"You know what I'm thinking?" Raoul says.

"No," she says in a slow lingering voice.

"I'm thinking we should have that shnickle you promised me."

"Good idea." Nadja reaches for her bag on the floor.

"But," Raoul continues. "What I was really thinking about was the soufflé last night."

"Me too," she exclaims, sitting up.

Raoul shoots her a glance. "See?" he says, and she nods. It is Raoul's way of saying that they are connected in ways that even they do not fully understand.

"Yes," she says, "I do."

They smoke the rest of the cigarette, and Nadja stretches out her legs on the dashboard, a pleasant buzz in her head. Soon, they will arrive at Sabine's, the proud owner of a small cottage on the North Fork, a cottage that Sabine and Nadja have named La Casa. The cottage is right on the Sound, and the water, most days, is beautiful and calm. Nadja is a regular visitor; Raoul, a first-time guest.

Nadja makes plans. "We'll jog and swim. We'll go bike-riding."

"Does she have bikes?"

"Of course," Nadja says smugly, as if she were the proprietor of the bikes and the cottage—being Sabine's friend entitles her. According to this line of logic, Raoul, invited to come along as Nadja's mate, should be grateful.

"Do you want to stop for coffee?" Raoul asks.

"No," she says, "let's just get there. Unless you want to stretch your legs," she adds with impromptu generosity.

"No, I'm fine."

She looks at him again, allowing tenderness into her heart. At forty-seven, he is eleven years her senior, and she feels sorry for him when she thinks about his other life. Originally from Argentina, now thirty years in this country, Raoul is a resourceful businessman with capital to his name, shared with Lydia, his wife. Sitting in the car, Nadja feels a little strange, maybe some guilt, occupying Lydia's lawful seat. Sometimes she has the weird, and thankfully brief, feeling that Lydia is in the car with them. Lydia, no doubt, had a say about the color, the make; it is probably she who read the consumer reports. Husband and wife went together to the car dealership in Rye, test-drove the car, discussed the various features they would have to pay extra for. Raoul once told Nadja that shopping with one's spouse was the least sexy of activities, but the way Nadja sees it, shopping with one's spouse is the connective tissue that binds them together and gives them this look, the couple's look. Indeed, Raoul and Lydia look alike—Nadja has seen photographs—they have the same smile, the same composure of features, whereas Nadja and Raoul do not look even remotely alike.

Nadja has no intention of "stealing" Raoul from his family but at times, when in a certain mood and feeling defeated, she experiences a bitter resentment toward Lydia, and even toward the kids; this frightens her, and she instantly repents. On the rare occasions when their fights reach a crescendo and her self-loathing is charged to the fullest, she mocks Raoul to his face, deriding his small, perfect life, his two kids, a boy and a girl, now in college and the exact replicas of papa and mama in their aspirations. "You're in the cloning business," she tells Raoul, and he, perhaps understanding more than he lets on, says nothing.

Once, as they were walking home on a cold night, Raoul let a whimsical thought cross his lips, wishing Lydia to vanish somehow. Both Nadja and Raoul were shocked. They stopped walking and looked at each other for a moment and then smiled, half embarrassed, half giddy with the profanity of such a thought. Then Nadja spat on the sidewalk against the evil eye and made Raoul do the same.

Nadja reaches for the seatbelt. Lydia, Raoul says, always wears it. Nadja and Raoul seldom do, but lately Nadja has begun to have flashes of a terrible car accident. The car turns over again and again, and she and Raoul require medical attention. The authorities get involved, and she and Raoul are found out: the scandal, the shame—their due punishment for being so careless and immoral. If they die, people will say they got what they deserved. People always know what others deserve.

Nadja looks at Raoul, his hands on the wheel, and bursts out laughing.

"What's funny?"

"You. A pilot."

He glances at her. "A pilot? Oh, yes," he recalls.

Last night, as Nadja was eating her dessert, allowing Raoul a taste, Raoul said, "I had the weirdest dream…"

Nadja gave him a look—he always starts like this when telling her his dreams—and he said, "All right, maybe not the weirdest, not in the top ten, but weird. I'm a pilot—"

"A pilot?!" Raoul is useless when it comes to mechanics. "Maybe a co-pilot?"

"No, I'm alone at the controls. It's a TWA plane—"

"Oh, the one that crashed."

He paused. "No, but it makes you wonder why TWA. Anyway, I'm waiting for takeoff on the runway—"

"Do you have passengers?"

"I don't remember, maybe. There are a couple of planes ahead of me, so I climb down and go for a walk. Then, walking back, I can't find my plane. I'm crossing a field and come to a house and knock on the door, and this man comes out and I say to him, 'Look, I'm a pilot…'"

By this point, Nadja was laughing hysterically, envisioning Raoul going up to a stranger and saying, Look, I'm a pilot…

"…I say to him, 'Look, I'm a pilot, but I can't find my plane.' But before that, as I'm crossing the field, I'm thinking I must ask one of the other pilots how far I should push the throttle for takeoff…"

"It must have been a wonderful feeling, being in charge of the plane and ready for takeoff," Nadja now says.

Raoul sighs. "It was, at first, but then I got anxious when I couldn't find my plane."

"And you never got to fly," Nadja adds ruefully.

"True, I never got to fly."

"Many guys say they fly in their dreams, like, you know, Superman, and without a machine. They just fly."

"Yes, I've had those dreams, too, but I think being a pilot carries more oomph and authority. Responsibility."

"Hmmm. You mean the passengers?"

"The passengers and the crew. And the machine, as you call it, is an expensive piece of equipment. You have to know how to operate it. You need a license."

"But then, why can't you find your plane? And why do you need to ask another pilot about the throttle?"

"Well, maybe I am some kind of a novice pilot, and maybe

it's my virgin flight. Maybe I'm just flying out to Long Long Island with my one and only Nadja and I worry about an accident, tfu, tfu."

"Tfu, tfu," Nadja echoes, spitting air.

And here, at last, is the gray cottage. They pull into the driveway behind Sabine's newly leased Honda. "Leather seats!" Sabine boasts when she gets the chance to rave about the car. Sabine, Nadja thinks, is a first generation nouveau riche par excellence, but with a certain charm, given Sabine's natural penchant for self-deprecation. An assortment of buoys hang from the back porch railing, and colorful wind socks merrily swing in the breeze. At first Nadja ridiculed the buoys and the socks as just another symptom of Sabine's burgeoning bourgeois soul, but now she finds she actually likes them.

And there, on the doorstep, are Sabine and Butterscotch: an adoring mistress in print shorts and shirt, and her impervious cat. Sabine has tons of clothes she shoves into her drawers and sort of hangs in her closets in no discernible order, and Nadja always wonders how Sabine finds or decides what to wear on any given day. Often, like this morning, her choices seem haphazard, and the ensemble of dissimilar prints offers a cacophony of colors and shapes. And yet, Sabine, in her schlumpy disheveled way, somehow manages to look snappy, at least in Nadja's eyes. Sabine's tan small feet are in rubber thongs.

Nadja and Sabine exchange blasé kisses and hugs—blasé on Sabine's part, Sabine who acquiesces to physical contact in a queer mixture of passivity and indifference. Instantly, if casually, Sabine appropriates Raoul to demonstrate for him the merits of her car, and Nadja, somewhat miffed, and yet willing Sabine and Raoul to "bond," schleps their bags from trunk to guest room. She puts away the foods that she and Raoul have bought that morning at the Gourmet Garage, complying with Sabine's demands. When one is invited to Sabine's, one is not exactly a guest: somehow or other one must pay. It has recently come out in a conversation that Sabine keeps a record on who has visited her, and for how long, so that she could mention it, as if in passing, when the time is right: "You spent five nights in my house this summer." Sabine has never said this to Nadja, but Nadja is waiting. She can just see Sabine's face, hear her voice, when she tells Nadja how many times she has been to the cottage, how privileged and indebted she should feel for knowing Sabine.

"What took you so long?" Sabine asks, and Nadja and Raoul look at each other.

"It took us two hours," Raoul says. "How long does it take you?"

"About the same, but I thought you'd get here sooner."

"We had to stop at the Gourmet Garage to get some stuff for you," Raoul says.

"Oh, you did?" Sabine is ecstatic. "Where is it?"

"In the fridge," Nadja says.

In the guest room, Nadja and Raoul strip off their clothes and Nadja, playfully, reaches for his package. It is a habit with her, a habit that still gives her pleasure, physical as well as mental, as if, with this small weighing gesture, she proclaims possession of him.

Raoul pushes her hand away, looking at the half-open door.

They change into their bathing suits and Nadja goes down to the beach and plunges into the cool water. Ah, the good life. Sabine, with her purple goggles and her red white and blue Olympics swimming cap, joins her. Sabine has an arsenal of caps, goggles, and colorful swimsuits, and today she is wearing a green suit, with a long, latticed V stretching down to her navel. At any given time, Nadja has only one suit, black, and one pair of goggles, also black.

Raoul, a bottle of Pete's Wicked Ale in his hand, waves from the porch.

"Why doesn't he join us?" Sabine asks.

Nadja regards Raoul through Sabine's eyes: male, middle-aged, a pair of old, red nylon swim trunks—definitely not cool; Nadja feels a bond with Raoul.

"He might, later."

"Is he a good swimmer?"

"He's not a water person, he's a beach-and-book person."

They swim parallel to the shore. The water is clear, refreshing. The sun is strong, but not too strong. Nadja dives, then floats on her back, looking at the very blue sky, wondering, not for the first time, what makes it blue. Is she enjoying herself? Yes, she is. And yet, she would have been just as happy had she stayed home. Around people she is usually tense, feeling compelled to display good cheer and humor.

Nadja resumes swimming. Sabine stands farther away, waiting for her. Sabine spits into her goggles.

"Why do you do that?" Nadja asks.

"To prevent the goggles from fogging up, you little ignorant you."

Nadja laughs. "Do you know what makes the sky blue?"

Sabine eyes her. "Is it very important?"

Nadja is intent on Sabine's mouth, the way Sabine's lips and teeth work together to produce her precise, bitchy-sounding enunciation; her feisty belligerence shines through, even when she is acting friendly. Biologically, Sabine is a woman in her forties, but she is, in fact, a baby, if a shrewd one, still fighting her childhood battles. She is self-conscious about her mouth— she won't smile if she can help it—because of her bunched up teeth. Nadja is surprised that Sabine's Jewish, well-to-do parents did not think to arrange for braces at the appropriate age.

"It's not important," Nadja says, "but I rely on you to tell me practical things. Do you think it's the water reflected in the sky?"

"If anything, it's the other way around. Water has no color."

"Neither does air."

"You ask the most inane questions." Sabine, languidly, draws half circles across the surface of the water, causing tiny splashes, and the expression on Sabine's face alerts Nadja to be ready. "What does he tell his wife when he goes off with you?"

Even with Sabine, Nadja feels uncomfortable discussing Lydia. It brings up the fact that Raoul is a liar and a cheat, and that Nadja, his accomplice, is not much better. She considers herself an honest person, and yet, her life is full of deceit, not only with Raoul, but also at the office. Like a thief, she constantly worries about getting caught.

"Oh, some business commitment," Nadja feigns a light tone.

"And she believes him?"

"It looks like she does. We don't do this very often, and they've been married for so long, I don't think she really cares. Maybe she is happy to have the house all to herself."

"I'm sure she knows. Women know these things. Do they fuck?"

"Not often. Long-term couples rarely do."

"How do you know?"

"He tells me. Not only he and his wife, but their friends, too. They have what they call the obligatory fuck once or twice a month."

"You're so naïve. Does it occur to you that Raoul may be lying to you?"

Sabine does this often. It is a principle with her to be challenging, mercilessly blunt. She is good at putting people like Nadja on the defensive and getting information out of them.

"He has no reason to lie to me. Besides, I'm not really jealous of his wife."

"Of course you are."

"I'm not, not when it comes to sex."

"Well, I still think that he must lie to you. Men always lie."

"I thought you liked Raoul."

"For a man he's all right, and he puts up with you. Years ago, I used to fuck men. I even liked a couple of them."

Nadja splashes water on her face; the sun, in fact, is very hot. She would rather swim than talk, but she can't think of a way to end the conversation without having Sabine accuse her of trying to avoid the subject, or of being rude. Not that Sabine could not take some rudeness. "So why don't you try a man for a change? I've always said you were a fake dyke."

"I don't want a penis in my life. Still, I can't believe his wife doesn't know."

"Maybe she does and is smart about it. Maybe she is glad to be released from sex duties."

"You said he was good in bed."

"He is for me, but maybe not for her, after so many years. He says she is not interested so much in sex anymore. He and his friends have a theory about sex and marriage, and they blame the wives. They say that women at a certain age dry up, something having to do with menopause and estrogen levels. I tell him it's bullshit, the wives are simply bored with the husbands. If they had the guts and took on a lover, they'd be rejuvenated in sex."

"Well, what about you? I don't understand how you can come with a guy you've been seeing for over two years."

Nadja laughs, and Sabine stops drawing circles in the water. Anxiously, she asks, "You work at it?"

"At what?"

"Coming."

Nadja hesitates. She can be honest, she can be evasive. Sabine is a gossip and whatever Nadja tells her, if juicy enough, will be repeated, distorted and enhanced, a dozen times as Sabine spreads the news among their friends. Nadja hates gossip, but she tolerates Sabine because Sabine comes right back and tells you what she said about you and what others said about you. And since Sabine discusses everyone with everybody, it is no longer a true case of gossip behind one's back, but a sort of net weaving that keeps them all well connected and informed, if a bit swampy.

"Of course," Nadja says.

"How?"

"I tense my muscles, I concentrate."

"And you breathe fast?"

Nadja has to think. "No, I actually stop breathing."

"You slut. Let's jog back. Be careful, though, there are small rocks here and there. I hurt myself last week."

They jog back, and Nadja, always worried about physical injury, is especially mindful of the rocks underfoot. Something she did not tell Sabine, and probably will not, is that lately she has been feeling discontented with Raoul and would gladly welcome a new lover, if only she met one. She feels sorry for herself, the way she hungrily looks at men on the street, even men who are not exactly her type, but may turn out to be her type. She looks at their crotch, trying to assess the goods, hoping that one day she will reach the heights of sex and love, if such a thing is at all possible. She longs for passion, for true and lasting partnership, something she has yet to experience. She is greedy, yes, but the hungry are always greedy.

Sabine is a bit ahead of her, and Nadja watches the short and determined figure, the bobbing Olympics-capped head. The sun is beating down, and Nadja is thinking skin cancer, she is thinking crime and punishment: she is a sinner, and she deserves punishment. At any moment, God may strike her dead. And even if God does not punish her, she is doing a good job of it herself. Death inhabits a permanent, if inelegant, corner in her mind; every day it makes its presence known. At this hour, if she were not here, at Sabine's, she would be at the office, maybe working on Woman, maybe doing slave-work. With a few exceptions, Nadja is the only person she knows who has a real job. Sabine, like most of her friends, is well-off and does not need to work: she is a Published Author and lives off a small inheritance her aunt has left her, as well as a monthly allowance from her parents. Nadja has published a couple of short stories and lives off her wages.

As she jogs, a sense of the eternal briefly visits her mind, immediately followed by sadness. To counter it, Nadja tells herself how beautiful the water is, how lucky she is to be where she is. Better not think about life, just live it. She deserves this respite. She should look forward to a cool beer, a cigarette, lounging under the awning on the porch, and schmoozing. This is what people do on nice summer days, people who can afford it, and she can afford it thanks to Sabine and Raoul.

"Wait for me," Nadja shouts, and Sabine stops. Approaching, Nadja begins to laugh.

"What is it?" Sabine asks.

"You. You look funny from behind."

"Funny, how?"

"You look like a boy, no, like a little man. An eager little man, very determined. Maybe a cap-wearing midget."

Despite herself, a burst of snorting laughter escapes Sabine. "I'm taller than you," she retorts, and they resume jogging toward the cottage, now in sight.

On the porch, Raoul sits with a novel he found on Sabine's shelves, *The Weekend*. Nadja is happy to see him read. She also remembers that she likes Raoul because he knows how to be quiet. She and Sabine are down on the beach, under an umbrella. Sabine is mildly despondent. Life is too hard, she says, and Nadja nods.

To make matters worse, Sabine says, she cannot stop scratching. For Nadja's benefit, she enumerates and points to various bruises, cuts, scars on her legs and arms. Some are credited to Butterscotch, others to unhappy encounters with furniture and miscellaneous hazards, such as her own nails in the middle of the night. Often she wakes, mindlessly scratching, unable to stop.

Indeed, Nadja notes with amazement, Sabine's skin is a mess, a collage of scabs and marks. "Go see a doctor," she says, and Sabine sighs. She has seen so many doctors, what's the point, they don't know what it is, or pretend to know what it is, you can never tell with doctors, some say it's an allergy, some say it's a systemic yeast infection. In the meantime, she scratches, and no one cares.

"Maybe it's all the pills and vitamins you take," Nadja offers. Looking at Sabine, she realizes once again that even though she knows Sabine, she does not really know her. Sabine reads all the health and diet books as soon as they appear on the market and she follows all of them in spurts. Sabine's mind, Nadja believes, just like Sabine's computer, is overburdened; Sabine reads the junk advice and retains too much of it.

"I hate everybody," Sabine says. "You're my only true friend, the only person I can trust."

Nadja is flattered.

"You must promise me you'll always be my friend, no matter what I do or say," Sabine continues.

"As long as you don't betray me." Nadja tries to sound demure and grave.

"You know, they say that writers are people with a grudge, but you don't seem to have any. You're so balanced."

Is this a compliment, Nadja wonders, or is Sabine implying that Nadja is not a real writer? Often, Nadja feels that Sabine is playing cat-and-mouse with her, testing her.

"Oh," Nadja says, "I have plenty of grudges."

"But you're secretive, you hide them well."

"I don't complain as much as you. I don't see the point."

"Talking is the point." Sabine puckers her lips. "If you don't complain, people think you act superior."

"What people?"

Sabine waves her hand. "I don't know, people. Someone said to me the other day you were acting superior."

"Who was it?"

"I don't remember."

"I think you're making this up."

"I'm not, I'm telling you, you come off superior, but what do I know? I haven't published a book in four years. When you don't publish, people assume you're finished, they don't treat you with respect. They think it is safe to ignore you. I need to publish a book that will make them all die of jealousy. Publishing a book is my only revenge against them. My only possible consolation. I was thinking recently about some writer, I now forget who, who became a celeb at a very young age, and it occurred to me that if you make it when you're young, the list of those who wronged you is relatively short. But if you make it when you're older, your list is satisfyingly long, and your sense of vindication much greater. Unless—" Sabine pauses, then continues. "Unless, once you make it, you no longer care about those lowlifes who were mean to you. Or, maybe the old gripes don't mean much anymore, but new ones arise. Maybe we delude ourselves into believing that if we make it, we'll attain nirvana."

"Only in the grave, maybe," Nadja says. "Besides, it's good to worry about things. When you worry and try to figure things out, your brain gets a workout."

"My brain gets enough of a workout. If it needs anything, it's complete rest," Sabine says. "I even worry about wrinkles in my earlobes. They do wrinkle in your sleep, you know."

Nadja laughs. "No, it never occurred to me," she says and, for a while, they say nothing, just contemplate the water. Nadja is thinking about revenge, about how she always vows not to judge people, telling herself to be open and accepting, but when she's

34

directly involved, when she feels that someone has deliberately wronged or insulted her, all resolutions lose their power, and she thinks of revenge, bitterly and miserably, knowing all the while that such thoughts only poison the soul. They're just noise in the brain, harmful noise that goes about its destructive work, bruising the already bruised soul.

Nadja thinks she should share this insight with Sabine, but then another thought strikes. "Still, you did make it when you were young."

Sabine sits up. "Not really. I mean, I was published in my twenties, but I didn't make it big. Maybe I'm being too hard on myself. My shrink says I should concentrate more on my accomplishments and less on my failures."

"Easier said than done," Nadja says philosophically. She wants to go in for a swim one more time before it gets dark, but she would have to pull herself together and get up on her feet, and, right now, it is so pleasant to just remain where she is, listening, sipping her second beer.

Now Sabine talks about love. "I'm so bored with everything. I feel like I should play the game, find a part-time lover, maybe once a week in the afternoon. I just need the stuff, I don't know why. Deep down I'm so … I don't know what I am deep down. I think I need something stronger than vanilla sex. I want someone I can sex with."

Nadja laughs. Someone to sex with. Someone to have chocolate sex with. Vanilla sex is probably the kind of sex she and Raoul are satisfied with, but Sabine's appetites are greater and harder to satisfy. Presumably, vanilla sex is the sex Sabine has had with Diane, her partner, now on a well-deserved leave from Sabine. They call it a trial separation, but Nadja has her doubts about the relationship. Nadja likes Diane—blonde, gentle, if a little cold in manner—but she is also happy to have Sabine to herself, if only because she and Sabine get along better when it's just the two of them.

"What's wrong with vanilla sex?" Nadja asks.

"It's too boring, I fall asleep in the middle. I haven't had a decent orgasm in months. I need something more extreme, I crave weird stuff, S&M. I want to go out and seduce women, buy them dinner and such. I want to find a stranger, someone I can pay for sex."

"You can pay me, I could use the money."

"No, not you, sweetie, someone who is into the stuff."

"Why do you want to pay?"

"So I can degrade her more, I suppose?" A slothful raising and dropping of the arm.

"Like a man," Nadja says.

"That's an insult," Sabine chides softly.

"No. Men have always had more money, they can pay for things."

From the porch, a big, audible yawn; Sabine and Nadja look up at Raoul.

"You know," Sabine says, "you have dyke energy. I can't imagine you with a man."

Nadja laughs, glancing up at the porch. "You think I'm a dyke?"

"All women are dykes." Sabine thoughtfully scratches a scar. "We got it all backwards. In New York people fuck for power, for careers, not for sex."

"I don't know about that," Nadja says. "Anyway, among bonobos, the males are subdued in the face of female solidarity; female bonding is secured by the friendly practice of genital rubbing."

"Makes perfect sense to me. And to you, too, I'm sure." Sabine looks at Nadja. "But what is it you like about Raoul?"

"I like…" Nadja lingers, putting her thoughts in order. "I like that he is practiced in love. He's practically enmeshed in it. There's his wife, his kids, his parents, his siblings. He's known love from day one. He loves."

They come out with their dinner plates and silver and set them on the round table on the porch. They are under the stars, feasting on grilled butterfly lamb, salad, corn on the cob, and wine from the local wineries. A constant sound effect: waves lapping at the shore. Moths and gnats are drawn to the single light above the grill, and every once in a while there is a popping sound when one of them is scorched. What happens to their little corpses, Nadja wonders. Do they turn to ash? Do they drop on the food on the grill?

Better not think about corpses and ashes. Idly, she considers the question of atmosphere, the sense of time turning heavy and dense all around them. It is quite magical, she decides, resting her head on the back of the chair and looking up at the fat stars in the deep, dark sky. It is all so peaceful, and yet hearts keep on beating. Soon enough she will be pushing her key in the lock and step into a dark apartment. She will prepare for bed, summarize the weekend as nothing gained, nothing lost. A nice weekend, and yet, in the end, nothing lasting. But, at least she is living, heeding Cendrars's: "Live, first of all, live. I am of the earth." Then Monday will come and it will be back to the grind, back to Jerry, back to feeling small and inconsequential.

Raoul compliments Sabine, "Everything is delicious, Sabine."

"It is," Nadja echoes, just to hear herself speak.

"I take good care of my guests," Sabine, now in a chirpy mood, declares.

"So Nadja tells me."

Why, Nadja wonders, is she thinking about Monday? When she was young, she could spend days and nights with friends, doing "nothing," drinking, getting high, shouting and laughing. Shouting, it now seems, was the thing: the louder, the more hysterical, the more alive she felt. These days, shouting does nothing for her, and only at her desk does she lose the sense of time, of herself. Often, when she looks at her calendar for the coming week and the pages are blank, she is glad she has no social commitments. But, now and then she suffers a momentary lapse and feels empty and sad for having no commitments.

Nadja lights a cigarette.

Sabine sighs. "Must you smoke?"

"Just a couple of puffs, I'll kill it in a minute."

Raoul, laughing, embarks on a story. "I have this friend, Karl, who has a healthy mistrust of the system. When he buys cigarettes, he counts them. And every time he counts them and there are twenty in the pack, he is appeased but also a little miffed that he hasn't caught them."

All at once, Sabine is animated. "I don't blame him. I could tell you a story, but if I did, you'd think I'm neurotic."

"We won't," Nadja promises, willing herself to be jolly and carefree and present in the moment.

"I take these pills, you know, for my thyroid? They're very tiny, you see, and every time I fill the prescription, it's hard to believe there are a hundred pills in the bottle, so one day I decide to count them, and guess what? I was right, there are only ninety-eight! I go downstairs and storm into the pharmacy, saying I've always known they're cheating me and now I have proof, and the Indian behind the counter comes out and pulls me aside, presumably to calm me down, but, in fact, to sequester me from the other customers. He puts the pills through this counting machine, and I begin to sweat, thinking that maybe I miscounted, and all I had achieved by coming in screaming like a lunatic is to make a fool of myself, but then the guy begins to apologize, saying that indeed there are only ninety-eight, he has no idea how such a thing could have happened. By now I'm utterly exhausted, and even feel sorry for the guy—he could lose his license, you know—I just take my pills and go home, but I won't be surprised if it's a common practice. I figure, if they cheat each customer out of a couple of pills, there's a nice profit right there, tax-free."

Raoul shakes his head and says, "Only in America."

"What do you mean?" Sabine asks suspiciously.

Nadja looks at Raoul. He is a bit self-conscious around her friends, her friends being artists, and he a mere businessman.

"This story, like the song," Raoul says and sings, "Only in America…"

Nadja laughs and punches him in the arm. "He is trying to be funny."

"Oh," Sabine says. "Of course, I've gone back there for medication and such, but I don't bother to count anymore, I proved my point. I don't like to think that I'm crazy."

Later, before they turn in, Sabine says to Raoul, "Feel free to make noise, you know, I actually like it."

Raoul glances at Nadja, then back at Sabine, and Nadja and

Sabine burst out laughing. "No, no, I don't mean sex, although that's fine too," Sabine explains. "I mean, in the morning. I don't get up at the crack of dawn like you guys, but I like to hear people moving about while I'm still kind of groggy and half asleep."

"Because you know they'll be making breakfast for you," Raoul says.

"Precisely."

In bed, Raoul and Nadja cuddle but nothing more. Sabine is in the next room, and Nadja knows that Sabine is listening. Sabine is shamelessly nosey, wittingly and unwittingly. Once, as Nadja was reaching orgasm, the telephone rang: it was Sabine on the line, speaking to Nadja's machine, ordering Nadja to pick up. It was odd, having sex with Raoul and listening to Sabine's voice, emptily floating in the living room, telling Nadja all that went wrong for her that day. Sabine leaves the longest messages. She will talk to a machine until the machine cuts her off. The next day, when Nadja told Sabine she was coming when Sabine called, Sabine was very pleased, like she had something to do with it. A few years ago, when Nadja first met Sabine, Sabine, not yet the owner of the cottage, was renting a lakefront cabin, and Nadja arrived for the weekend. The next morning, upon waking, Nadja heard a strange, rhythmic sound coming from Sabine's bedroom. As the sound persisted, Nadja grew increasingly curious, only to find out later that while she was busy imagining all sorts of kinky scenarios, Sabine was innocently typing her dreams on the laptop.

ll we do is eat," Nadja says, looking at the sourdough baguette, the cheeses, the smoked salmon and capers from the Gourmet Garage. Only a minute ago she was starving and, sitting down at the table, she even thought with delight: how wonderful it is to be hungry and have good food laid out before you.

"Do I hear a complaint?" Sabine asks.

"No, not yet," Nadja says.

"But it's true," Sabine continues, "Americans eat too much. We're the most obese nation in the world."

"And wasteful, too," Nadja adds.

"I don't know about you guys," Raoul says, "but I'm hungry." He reaches for the bread and breaks a hefty piece of the crispy baguette.

"Me too, in fact." Sabine giggles.

"Dostoevsky said that the best definition of man is a being who walks on two legs and is ungrateful."

"So?" Sabine and Raoul say in unison.

"So, nothing," Nadja says. She would love to light a cigarette, stretch out her legs on the table and be nineteen again, acting and feeling bohemian, or that's what they used to call it when she was nineteen. She took her time growing up for far too long and now feels she must hurry and catch up with things—before she knows it, she'll be forty. The years sneak up on you, her mother and her mother's friends used to say, a certain look on their faces. They sounded sage when they said it, and Nadja listened but never took it to heart because such a thing could never happen to her. But too often now she finds herself looking back, wondering about the seemingly alien and distant years that came and went without her noticing. She wants to recapture and make sense of the whole mass, of her history, insubstantial and yet weighty. Right now, though, she is willing to let go and just stretch out her legs and light a cigarette but she knows she would be castigated or banished from the table, for cigarettes are no longer glamorous, and thrusting your feet in people's faces while they eat is unacceptable behavior around so-called grownups.

"Here." Raoul hands her a piece of baguette smeared with cheese and a slice of salmon on top. "This will get your juices flowing."

"Thanks." Chewing the bread and cheese and salmon, Nadja, to add yet another flavor to the mix, reaches for a locally grown tomato and bites into it, and then takes a sip of the delicious aromatic French roast blend. At home she does not bother with brewing coffee, she drinks instant.

"Good?" Raoul asks, and she nods.

"You're too nice to her," Sabine mutters.

"So are you," says Raoul.

"You know something, I never thought about it quite this way. You're right! I am too nice to her."

Nadja laughs. "You should see your face," she tells Sabine.

"What's the matter with my face?"

"It looks extremely worried."

"Well, of course. I don't like to think I'm too nice to people, it's pathetic. Some good souls respond to kindness with kindness, but most people respond with contempt. I speak from my own experience. Even my shrink says I'm too soft. He says I should toughen up, that I should be ruthless. He says that in order to succeed, artists must be ruthless."

"You're ruthless enough," Nadja says. "Still, I must be doing something right if both of you are nice to me. Maybe I'm nice to you?"

"Is she nice to you?" Sabine turns to Raoul.

Raoul looks at Nadja and then Sabine, too, looks at Nadja. Nadja feels a bit ill at ease. She wonders if Raoul, because of Sabine, will try to say something witty.

"She is," Raoul says. "When she's in a good mood. And she is also the most generous person I know."

"Really?" Sabine is surprised. "You're just saying that because you want to please her."

"Not true. She's heard it before, she knows what I think."

"Raoul is the only person who really knows me," Nadja says.

"I knew you'd say that," Sabine says. "I'm very generous myself, I just don't show it."

They laugh. "But you do let show your competitive side," Nadja says. "Even with me."

Now they are all busy chewing, and Nadja looks over at the water. They are a family of sorts. Two women and a man, sharing breakfast on the porch. Sabine eats with an attitude, with a certain nonchalance that Nadja always finds very affecting. Sabine eats as if she could not care less about the food, or how it tastes. She acts unhurried, as if not worried that the others may get to eat more than their share. She reaches for the bread, the salmon, arm and hand sort of dangling, but, ultimately, very precise, never dropping anything, as Nadja expects her to, never breaking anything. Nadja, on the other hand, broke a couple of expensive glasses—here in the cottage and in Sabine's loft in the city. It is curious, because Nadja normally does not break things.

"Did you feed Butterscotch?" Sabine remembers to ask.

"Of course." Nadja crunches into another baguette sandwich; Raoul was right, she is hungry. "We had a small tête-à-tête, Butterscotch rubbing against me and mewing breakfast, not letting Raoul come near me."

"I have to say," Raoul says. "I'm not a cat person, but even I can tell that Butterscotch is special."

"He's a pain, if you want to know the truth," Sabine says, "but he has a soul, which I can't say for many people I know."

"I don't know why but I thought he was a she," Raoul says.

"Well, he-she, it's all the same in this house."

"I see."

Who am I? Nadja thinks. Sitting here, like a real person, with Sabine and Raoul?

"I don't think cats have souls," Raoul says after a pause.

"How would you know," Sabine says with so much disdain, the three of them nearly choke on their food with laughter. Earlier, waiting for Sabine to wake up, Nadja and Raoul lay together on a lounge chair on the porch, drinking coffee from a large mug and watching the water. Nadja told herself she was feeling serene, content, and yet a small voice in her head reminded her that such states do not last. She wondered what it would be like to have Raoul wake up at her side every morning: would they love each other more, or would they get on each other's nerves?

"…It's so frustrating dealing with such people," Sabine says, completing a complaint about some electrician who tried to cheat her out of eight hundred dollars.

"Tell me about it," Raoul, the homeowner, says.

Actually, Nadja now recalls, Sabine did break a vase this past winter in Nadja's apartment. Nadja had invited a few friends for dinner, and Sabine kept disappearing in the bedroom, disrupting the guests and the flow of the evening. Nadja was annoyed, thinking that Sabine was probably snooping in there, when suddenly they heard something crash to the floor. Nadja rose from the table and went into the bedroom where, just like a kid, Sabine came up to her and began to cry, saying she was hiding in the bedroom because she was depressed and could not stand the company of people, and then, looking for something to do, she picked up the vase and it somehow dropped from her hand. Cleaning up the mess, Nadja tried to summon compassion for Sabine, but could not. She was too angry, even if she did not show it and was busy reminding herself that, aside from the mess and the annoyance of dealing with it, the broken vase was not much of a loss. She went back to her guests, and soon Sabine, who had gone into the bathroom, sat down at the table and continued to eat as if nothing had happened.

"It's a beautiful day," Raoul says, and they nod and look out to the water. At this hour, it is a clear, blue sheen, almost too blinding to look at. They should have gone bike riding, Nadja remembers. They should have gone yesterday afternoon or early this morning; now it is already too hot. Maybe later in the afternoon. Tomorrow she and Raoul will get in the car and drive back to the city on the long Long Island Expressway. To avoid traffic, Raoul will want to leave early, and she will sulk, but will finally agree. It feels as though they have just arrived, and already it is almost time to leave. She could, if she wanted to, let Raoul go back alone and stay here a little longer, even call in sick Monday morning, but for what end? Eventually she will have to go back to her life, which would not be so bad were it not for her job. As it is, she is chained to the calendar, pettily grateful for civic holidays.

In the kitchen, Raoul and Nadja do the dishes, while Sabine changes into her bathing suit. Raoul and Nadja kiss.

"You have good kisses, baby."

Nadja feels pampered. "You have to be nice to me."

"I am nice to you."

"Nicer."

After a climb of three flights of stairs, she is finally home: Twelfth Street and Avenue C. It is a small, rent-controlled one-bedroom, and the rent, nearly $700 a month, is still a bargain. She is sort of emotionally attached to this place, she has been calling it home for a number of years, but she does not like the thought that she may die here, in this small, quasi-renovated tenement apartment. The neighborhood has been changing and is actually becoming a desirable area—she is lucky to pay so little in rent. The worst feature: a persistent odd smell in the hallways and staircase. Some of her neighbors, mostly older men, seem weird, withdrawn. When she meets them downstairs at the mailboxes, or on the stairs, they look to the ground and mumble something, a greeting, she hopes. One of them, the one who looks like Charlie Manson, stopped her one day and told her that anarchy must begin at home: they must burn down the stinking debris of the so-called social order. When Nadja has nothing better to do, she worries that one day he will set fire to the place, and they will all go up in smoke.

She waters her plants, welcomes a new philodendron leaf, still tightly wrapped around itself, so virginally, delicately green. She loves this plant, it has grown under her care these past fifteen years. When she bought it, for a quarter, it was just one shoot in a small plastic container. Now it is a huge plant in a large clay pot on a tall stand. Whenever she goes past it, she intentionally brushes against the long-armed leaves for the soothing illusion that the plant reaches for her. Gently, she touches the new leaf, blows air on it. It looks like a newborn baby, all swathed and blind and trusting.

As predicted, Monday morning arrives and, somberly staring at her image in the old spotted mirror, the familiar feeling of futility and resentment sets in. Her clothes are all wrong—black cotton pants, a short-sleeved white shirt, espadrille sandals. In her private, everyday life she manages to look au courant, but dressing for work is a real struggle. She admires the goddesses she sees on the street, their breezy skirts and dresses, their high heels, their sheer, expensive stockings adhering to the leg like a brilliant breathing skin. She imagines their meticulous, dust-free closets; she covets the flair and the patience it takes to maintain a wardrobe. How she wishes she could look like them, but since she cannot afford the real expensive stuff, and since she lacks the dedication and ardor, she does not stand a chance. And so, every morning of a workday, she finds herself in the no-man's land between the casual and the formal, trying to improvise a solution that may work to her advantage. But such an improvisation always fails her, achieving nothing for her face or her figure, not to mention her state of mind.

This is no good way to start a day: if she does not like what she sees, why should others? She turns this way and that, pulling here, pulling there, smiling, posing, hoping to force a miracle. This is not me, she grumbles at her reflection, and yet it is the same "me" that will take her out to the street and down the subway. The "me" that will spend the entire day in an environment that is detrimental to one's mental health, and will pretend to do her job, a job not designed for her specifically. In fact, she was designed for it. The design is time-proven and perfect, whereas she, mere flesh and blood, is transient, incomplete. But, after all is said and done, she must fit in, and to a certain degree she has managed it, having learned to adjust and get along with her fellow-workers, just as they, no doubt, had to learn to adjust to her.

Cautiously, reluctantly, she steps out of the private and into the public. The "I" that loomed large, if miserable, indoors, now shrinks, to make room for others. A mild melancholy, which is to be expected, descends like a diaphanous web. Her spirit rebels, she does not want to go where she is going, but the body knows best: she must eat. Just like all the others who now hurry past her on the street, going to work. She identifies with the chickens, impaled on skewers, dripping fat and juices in the supermarket display-window. "Poor little chickens," she murmurs, as she stops for a moment to watch them. The roasting apparatus is old and rusty and each rotation ends with a clank. Poor little chickens, and yet so tasty when she is hungry; she moistens her lips.

It is a beautiful day, the sun is shining brightly, yet everyone, including Nadja, disappears in the depths of the transit system. We must love one another or die, said the poet, but Nadja—squashed on all sides by people taller than she—is fighting back tears of exasperation and rage. The noise level is unbearably high, and it feels as though everyone is in a surly, gloomy mood. There are such days when it seems that all of them have lost something they will never recover. There are such days when she wishes she had the nerve to let go and lose it in public, shouting and venting, breaking down before the astonished eyes of her fellow riders. They do not know her, they may assume this is usual behavior for her, even if she looks normal enough. Or looked normal enough until she opened her mouth and began to bawl. Some may pity her, others will look on, detached, at this lunatic who is screaming and yelling and sobbing, until some responsible person will finally summon the authorities, and she will be wheeled away on a stretcher to Bellevue. As the halcyon name suggests, they must have nice views of the East River, to soothe and calm the nerves of the incarcerated patients.

She thinks of those royal others, ensconced in the back seat of a gleaming sedan, driven by a chauffeur to their place of business. It is a world apart, shielded from them, the masses, behind tinted glass. Thinking such thoughts, a funny sensation stirs in Nadja, and she hears the cry of the historically oppressed. She understands revolutions; she has been waiting for one for many years now. Indeed, she feels like a leper those royal others must guard from.

Grand Central. She marches underground—a dwarf among dwarfs under the zodiac constellations depicted on the ceiling. How humiliated she feels having to do this, day after day, week after week, year after year. She knows it is absurd of her to feel this way, millions like her schlep to work every day, but the implied passivity in "employee" gnaws at her. Under the vaulted ceiling, the lot of them is reduced to a maze of feet, maneuvering briskly; as much as they hate their jobs, they all rush to get there. They have turned us into automatons, Nadja reflects. There are so many of us, we are the salt of the earth; were it not for us, there would be no economy, no old or new money.

She hates to admit it, but, like Woman, her protagonist, she wishes for someone to appear and lift her out of her life. A knight on a white horse. A knight in a white limo. Woman likes to fantasize that a man in the backseat of a limo glimpses her attractive silhouette as she walks down the avenue. He tells his driver to stop, jumps out of the car and approaches her—politely, reverently. Nadja has given this fantasy to Woman, while she herself, so she believes, is more realistic. Nadja knows that people in limos never notice a girl on the street. For such people, the rest of humanity is a blur, or worse, a stain; only the poor and hungry, Nadja is convinced, have the eyes and hearts for life. For life in its raw and elemental richness. Besides, Nadja hates limos. She hates what they represent and is repulsed by their naked vulgarity as they slink by among the other cars on the road. So, just a knight then, on foot.

She keeps her eyes on the ground, as if mesmerized by the assortment of sandals, shoes and sneakers, crisscrossing and racing every each way. She prides herself on her agility and urban knowhow, steering clear of the others, while keeping up a good pace. When she emerges in daylight, she takes a deep breath, remembering, too late, she would be breathing in unbreathable air, now dense and stagnant after the air-conditioned coolness below. She begins to cross the street, but quickly retreats, disbelieving her eyes. A man, wielding a long, machete-like knife, jumps out of a car and runs ahead toward another car, now stopped at the light. I knew it, she thinks, I should have stayed home. She turns back on her heels, trying not to think about the man with the machete.

What a way to start the week. A small voice tempts her to take the train and go back to bed, or, better yet, go to Brighton Beach with a six-pack.

She goes up another street; ultimately, all roads lead to the office. She enters the gray building, feeling relief and a powerful urge to cry. Upstairs, she says, "Hi," to Betty and Colleen, already seated at their stations, sipping their coffees. Betty, the only Hispanic on the floor, does not seem her usual self. It could be Jerry, it could be Betty's husband who, rumor has it, is quick with his fists.

She sits down at her desk. Her desk. She should have more feelings for something that is hers, for something she sits at five days a week. It is just a piece of furniture, an all right looking brown desk. She could make good use of it at home, but here, just like everything else, it only reminds her where she is. Sipping her coffee, she notes that Phil is not in his cubicle, which means he is in with Jerry, conferring. These two love to confer, which annoys her no end for the implicit accusation that she, the research assistant, does not confer enough with her boss. But, as long as Jerry is kept busy, she cannot complain, she is free to turn on her computer and access Woman.

Her intercom beeps. "You're late." Jerry is irritated.

"I know," she says, "I'm sorry."

"What's your excuse this morning?" Jerry hangs up, not waiting for a reply.

The prick, she mutters, pushing her USB into the port. She concentrates on the screen, ever alert to what goes on around her. For camouflage, and to give her corner a busy look, she spreads on her desk a couple of legitimate work files, and several pages of the Efficiency Report, the report that Jerry is waiting for. True, she is consistently late, five minutes or so every morning, proceeding according to a thought-out plan. If she is a few minutes late, takes a seventy-minute lunchbreak, spends time in the bathroom throughout the day, and, when possible, leaves a couple of minutes before five, she gains extra minutes of stolen freedom. And since she usually manages to sneak a few hours a day working on Woman, she ends up doing legitimate library work only two or three hours a day, and so manages to alleviate the feeling of being used by a cold and dehumanizing system.

Woman, a tax lawyer, is also at work. Woman has an office of her own, on the top floor of a modernist office building in the West Fifties. Woman, too, hates her job, but she enjoys the perks. She likes the title Attorney, and feels powerful when she is on the telephone, speaking to a client and leaning luxuriously against the soft leather of her executive chair. Every so often she swivels around to face the view of the tall buildings outside her wall-wide window, a view that fills her with gratitude but also anxiety. Nadja knows this woman's fantasies, her thoughts and grand hopes, yet she remains a little distant from her. She bodes her well, but is aware that Woman is willful, unpredictable, and on shaky ground, even if Woman chooses not to admit it. It occurs to Nadja that she may be as blind as her protagonist.

Her phone rings. "How are you, sweetheart?"

"I'm all right." She hears static on the line. "Where are you?"

"In a car," Raoul says, "on my way to New Jersey. One of my customers sent a company car for me."

Nadja stifles a sigh and remembers the man with the machete. It occurs to her that Raoul is one of those royals in the back seat of a sedan.

"At least you're getting around," she says. "How come he sent his car?"

"He wants me to see his plant."

"What kind of plant?"

"He makes parts for umbrellas."

"Umbrellas! Must be exciting."

Raoul laughs. "For him it is. He is very proud of what he's accomplished. He employs over two hundred people, they depend on him. That's what you don't understand about business. It is all about people, about people making a living. How's work?"

"I don't know. I wish I were in a company car, going to New Jersey. Why didn't you call me? I would have gone with you."

"Are you serious?"

"No." Nadja is gazing at Woman who is pacing in her office, thinking, tapping the eraser tip of a pencil to her forehead. "I have to go, darling."

"You called me darling."

She smiles. "I know."

"You haven't called me darling in a while. I'll see you tomorrow?"

"Tomorrow. Get me an umbrella."

"He doesn't make the umbrellas, only the parts."

"Ah, well, no umbrella. I don't like umbrellas anyway."

B ack from lunch, Nadja notices that Jerry's door is shut, which means he is either out to lunch, or in a closed-door meeting. Good! Nadja thinks as she settles down at her desk. She can prolong her lunch hour a little longer. But then she sees Betty walking toward her, a peculiar expression on her face. Betty glances at Jerry's door, and quickly whispers: "He's been on the phone with the Angel of Death for a long time. I have a bad feeling, Nadja. I think they are discussing you."

Nadja nods in thanks and, her heart beating, she watches Betty walk back to her desk. The Angel of Death on the phone with Jerry. The Angel of Death in the compact form of Mrs. Cooper from Human Resources. When she appears on a floor it means someone is about to get fired, and Nadja, as always, is the perfect candidate.

A strange sensation claims her—maybe fear, maybe panic—and she is suddenly cold all over. Tumult and clarity battle for space. Not so much fear of losing her job, but fear of the spectacle that awaits her, having to confront both Jerry and the Angel of Death. Maybe indeed this is Judgment Day. The day she has hoped for and dreaded for some time. Nadja reminds herself of the motto she has taught herself to summon when despair is lurking: Whatever happens happens for the best. But no motto can mitigate the humiliation she will have to endure, facing Jerry and the Angel of Death. And her heart, her poor heart, is beating and her eyes are burning.

Nadja tries to concentrate on her breathing, taking long steady breaths. She looks at her two idle hands, spread out on the desk, palms up. The gesture of supplication. She turns them over, and now observes the network of veins, the naked fingernails. Maybe she should apply nail polish, like most working women. Bright red or pink. Or even dark brown. Women who wear nail polish and blow-dry their hair do not have to fear Human Resources.

Human Resources. It used to be Personnel Department, which had a touch of the personal, of the person, in it. Now it is resources. Human, as opposed to mineral. Nadja would like to know who came up with this lofty, modern-sounding term. Probably some up-and-coming boy-genius during a staff meeting. And, like all other inanities, the term was adopted and spread like a plague. The Human Resources Department, embodied in the shape of Mrs. Cooper, is mobilized only when the coup de grâce is to be administered to the disgraced head of a fallen employee.

This is it, then, the moment of Corporate Climax and the inevitable discharge. Nadja looks over her desk, having to decide what she will need to pack if indeed Mrs. Cooper arrives on the floor and they fire her. Meantime, should she turn to her computer and pretend to be working? To spite, she could work on Woman during the very last moments while still on the payroll. Maybe just this once, she should treat her colleagues to an exclusive reading, pick out select passages from Woman and read them out loud. Let it be her swan song. Something for them to remember her by. Not a bad idea. A slave set free, she can now explore the limits of freedom in the office, allowing her true character, her true person, to break through in true-to-life dimensions.

She inserts her USB, and Woman, her loyal consort and possibly the source of her imminent problem, appears on the screen. Nadja gazes at the neat straight lines of words, determined to cast aside Jerry and Angel and focus her attention on Woman. A wasted effort; her brain and her fingers remain inert, and she is robbed of precious time, precious time.

Something—her sixth sense?—sounds an alarm in her head and she presses a key and her lovely screensaver appears. Then it is Jerry's voice, sudden and disturbing, right behind her.

"Ah, that screensaver again. It's curious, Nadja. Every time I come near you, the screensaver appears."

For a change, she is at a loss for words, totally unprepared for him, and yet weirdly attuned to every word, especially the implied intimacy of "come near you." Indeed, he is standing so close, she has no choice but to breathe in the sharp odor of soap, which sickens her, worrying that the odor would linger on her skin, in her nostrils, for hours. Jerry, she imagines, is one of those men who furiously lather themselves in the shower; it must make him feel clean and vigorous.

She stares at the colorful shapes, gracefully undulating on the screen. They are quite soothing; hypnotizing, in fact. She could let herself be mesmerized watching them, but Jerry is still leaning over her shoulder, breathing. There must be a law, she reflects, that mandates the appropriate physical distance a manager must keep from his subordinates. From where he stands, Jerry could easily push a key on her keyboard to retrieve her text, but he does not. Maybe there is still some decency left in the man, or maybe he is just toying with her, prolonging this delicious moment of suspense.

"I'm beginning to suspect, Nadja, it has something to do with me. Is it possible, do you think, that my presence manipulates your system?"

As "manipulate" and "system" hammer in her head, she tries, in vain, to come up with a witty answer, but a sudden weariness of body and mind dictate a flat reply. She swivels in her chair to face him, forcing him to step back. "I don't know, Jerry. It could be a coincidence." She sounds tired and old, a hundred years old.

"A coincidence, yes. Come into my office, please."

Instantly, she is alert. She must exit the file and put the USB in her bag before she leaves her desk. "Give me a minute, Jerry, I'll be right there."

"No, Nadja, I need you to come with me."

Slowly, reluctantly, she rises from her chair, hoping for some miracle, the small miracle of an urgent phone call from his wife, or some business matter Jerry would have to attend to immediately, forgetting all else. As if in a daze, she follows in his self-important footsteps into his office. What if Phil, a co-conspirator, goes over to her desk and confiscates the USB and Woman with it?

"Sit down, Nadja." Magnanimously, Jerry gestures toward a

chair as he goes around his desk and sits down. "Maybe we can talk? Like two adults?"

"Certainly." She manages to produce a little smile, to show Jerry that everything is as it should be and that even though she has no clue as to what they need to discuss like two adults, she looks forward to it.

And yet, she is jittery, she can hardly sit still, imagining Woman in Phil's defiling hands; she will have to beg to get the USB back. It is her only copy, but, luckily, they do not know this. She does have a copy on her hard drive at home, but it is not up-to-date. It is always the small things that get you in the end. She should have updated her file at home every night, just as she had told herself again and again, but, more often than not, she found excuses not to. She always updated the file on weekends, but not this past weekend. How could she have been so complacent? And the man with the machete. She should have followed her instincts and gone back home rather than come here so dutifully.

"You're smart, Nadja. I have a feeling you know what I'm about to say."

Smart? Did he actually say "smart?" "Smut?" Nadja observes the reddish mustache. And why does he have a feeling that she knows what he is about to say? Did Phil the snitch tell him that he had seen Betty whispering to her, probably telling her about Jerry speaking with the Angel of Death? If this is the case, Betty, too, will be punished somehow, and Nadja prays that whatever Jerry is up to, it is just his way of baiting her, saying in effect that she must know that she is guilty of something, and it is time to confess. But why would he even bother? Unless they have not reached a point of no return, and Jerry is about to offer her a trial period of sorts, a last chance to redeem herself.

Glumly, she shakes her head, but keeps her mouth shut; the less she says, the better, and the sooner she will be out of his office, a chastened employee or an employee no more.

Jerry explains, "As I've told you before, Nadja, on numerous occasions, if you want to stay with us, you'll have to try harder."

She nods.

"That's it, just a nod? Suddenly stingy with words?" He is smiling at her, his eyes aglitter. "I thought words were your forte."

He looks and sounds so absurd, she wants to let her jaw drop and stare at him in disbelief. Instead, she smiles. "Sure, Jerry, you are right, I'll have to try harder."

"You know what I mean by trying harder?"

"I think I do."

"All right, Nadja, tell me what I mean."

Pretending to think, she knits her brows and blows out some air, audibly. "I should get here on time."

"Good start, Nadja. What else?"

"Be more cooperative. Seek your advice more often," she says, deleting *and laugh at your and Phil's off-color jokes.*

"Yes, Nadja. What else?"

It begins to grate on her nerves, the way he keeps intoning her name; it never occurred to her before that her own name could sound so sinister. He is reeling her in, the bastard, trying to get something out of her. Maybe he is recording the conversation, which, as far as she knows, would be illegal. At any rate, whatever game he is playing, she feels she has said enough.

She looks up to the ceiling, again pretending to be deep in thought, then says, "I think I just about covered it."

But Jerry does not think so. "Come on, Nadja, I need you to be honest with me, and with yourself," he adds, almost cajoling, even imploring.

Momentarily, his gentle tone confuses her, and she recalls a dream of a few months ago where Jerry is very gentle and friendly with her. She is almost seduced to believe that he is sincere, but even in the dream she knows better. He employs this friendly tone when he needs to make it harder for her to lie; the snake knows a thing or two about employee psychology.

"But I am, I'm always honest with you," she says, letting real frustration edge into her voice. What is she doing here, battling this man? She should be at home, at her desk, working on Woman.

"So tell me a little about what you do all day. You seem so busy, so preoccupied. If I didn't know better, I'd think you were one hundred percent dedicated to us."

"But I am. There are the various reports I prepare for you and Phil, in addition to the day-to-day flow of issues I need to address. This takes time and mind power, as I'm sure you know."

"I know, Nadja, I know. I mean your other work. Please don't lie to me."

"I'm not lying to you."

Jerry sighs. "Okay, you're not lying." So nice, so gentle, just like a father. "I don't want to argue with you, Nadja."

"I don't want to argue, either." Again she tries to appear friendly, if reserved, but feels as though she is squirming in her seat, confirming Jerry's suspicion that she is guilty. This is the stuff good managers are made of, and she often wonders how they manage to be so coldly conniving and ruthless with their lessers, while also maintaining a fawning posture vis à vis their superiors. Presumably, it is all just a game, the trickle down of devious despotism, and this is what separates the so-called men from the boys, but, deep down, they must know they are nothing but posturing shells, toeing the line and holding on to their jobs, to their competitive position in the food chain.

Jerry picks up a paperclip and proceeds to mangle it. Systematically. Nadja observes his shiny nails, a part of her annoyed that he is destroying a good paperclip. She sits there, waiting, hoping that maybe Jerry is done with her, but then he says, "Just tell me about your other work. We all know that you do it, on company time, no sense denying."

"What do you mean, 'we all?'" She is bitter. "How come I don't know what you all know?"

"It's your own doing, Nadja, you're out of the loop. That's what I mean by trying harder. You have to try harder if you want to be in the loop."

Nadja nods. She wants to say she is in a different loop, several loops, in fact, the entire city is made of loops, some wider than others, some connect thanks to one or two people, forming clusters of friends, communities, not unlike galaxies and satellites in space. She could suggest to Jerry that it would be interesting to draw these clusters and loops over a New York City map, but Jerry would not appreciate it.

"I don't know exactly what type of work you do," Jerry is saying, "but I can only hope it's nothing that could get us all in trouble."

Get them in trouble?! Puzzled, she looks at him, trying to formulate a question, but before she can say anything, Jerry continues, conversationally. "You see, Nadja, we're not stupid, we know all that we need to know. Remember the mysterious page Phil found in the Xerox machine?"

"I already told you, it wasn't mine," she says, if a bit too fast. A page from Woman that got stuck in the bowels of the machine a couple of weeks ago and she could not retrieve it.

"Yes, it was," Jerry says softly, nearly absentmindedly, as he consults his watch. "What I'm trying to tell you is this." Jerry straightens up in the chair and pulls at the knot of his tie. "Mrs. Cooper should be here momentarily. We need to go over a few things with you. Why don't you go back to your desk? I'll call you in when she arrives."

A t her desk, Nadja checks to see if her USB is still in the port—relief! She quickly ejects it and puts it in her bag. What else? Nothing. All she can do now is wait. She could go to the bathroom, but she decides not to: both Betty and Colleen are not at their desks, so they may be in the bathroom, possibly embarrassed on her behalf, possibly discussing her fate at the hand of the dreaded Angel of Death. Phil seems to be hard at work, as if nothing out of the ordinary is taking place. And he is right. Nothing out of the ordinary. Just an employee getting shafted. And it is entirely the employee's fault. She is living proof that some women, women like her, are maladjusted, allowing their inflated egos to dictate their actions, instead of quietly acquiescing and getting on with the program, conforming to the natural order.

She turns to her computer and accesses the Efficiency Report. Let them find it on her screen after she has been dealt with and sent away. A good and conscientious employee until the very end. Maybe a trifle off in certain respects, but also efficient and fundamentally responsible.

What else? Maybe read a nice little poem to cleanse her brain of toxins produced by angels and efficiency reports. Yes, good idea! She reaches into her bag and brings out a recent purchase:

a volume of selected poems by Gwendolyn Brooks. As if it were a Bible, she opens the book at random, looking for her fate, and comes upon the lines:

> But I say it's fine. Honest, I do.
> And I'd like to be a bad woman, too,
> And wear the brave stockings of night-black lace
> And strut down the streets with paint on my face.

Indeed! Nadja's heart expands and she looks up, a happy smile of wonder on her lips. But, here comes Mrs. Cooper, prim and proper in her perennial dark suit, the globular rump imprisoned in tight pantyhose and skirt. Nadja shuts the book and openly watches Mrs. Cooper advance toward Jerry's office. She imagines that Mrs. Cooper's inner thighs rub together as she walks; in fact, she wouldn't be surprised to learn that Mrs. Cooper suffers from a rash and needs to powder her thighs before stuffing them in her nylon pantyhose. A serious-looking leather briefcase dangles from her hand. A briefcase that holds people's lives in it, confidentially. Sensible black pumps draw the eye to the thick ankles, now marching in a straight line to Jerry's office; she doesn't even glance in Nadja's direction. Mrs. Cooper, just like Jerry, has learned to muster a resolute, executive step.

She is not being fair—Mrs. Cooper is only doing her job.

Well, yes, maybe, but she does it with a vengeance.

The Angel of Death pulls the door shut behind her, and a suspenseful hush falls over the floor. Like in the movies, minus the swelling music. Presently, the door opens and Nadja is beckoned into Jerry's office.

Nadja cannot help it, she walks in with a broad, probably too broad, smile. Her heart is beating much too fast, and her mind is racing everywhere and nowhere. The Angel of Death, she reminds herself, cannot kill, only fire. But, she has been found out: she does not belong in decent society. Indeed, she may have gone a bit too far, and losing this job may be the beginning of the end. One small mistake, and one's whole world is overturned; it is too late now to retrace her steps and offer a new face, a new Nadja.

To her surprise, Phil is in the room, too, occupying his usual chair, with Angel sitting at his side. Another chair has been added; it is vacant, waiting for Nadja—the electric chair. The gang of three seems connected by something that makes them look charged and very much alive, more so than usual.

Three against one? And what is Phil doing there? A witness for the prosecution? The court reporter?

She sits down, crosses her legs, as if ready for a pleasant chat. She directs her smiling face at Jerry, aloof and solemn behind his desk, and then at Mrs. Cooper. Briefly, Mrs. Cooper's makeup catches Nadja's eye. It is very similar in style and color scheme to the makeup Nadja saw a girl apply this morning in the subway. The girl, oblivious to all, took out her kit and step by meticulous step proceeded to paint her face with brushes, pencils and other implements. A secretary, Nadja surmised, just starting out. Mrs. Cooper, too, began her career in the firm as a secretary; she made all the right moves, said all the right words, and was slowly and laboriously promoted to her current position. She may yet go far. Farther than Jerry.

Nadja puts her cold hands in her lap, looking friendly, innocent, as if she is here for a job interview, unaware of any drama. To distract herself, she idly wonders if the Angel of Death has ever been apprised of her sobriquet, and, if not, should Nadja do Angel the honor. In the meantime, she comports herself with civility. Smiling, she asks, "How are you, Mrs. Cooper?"

Mrs. Cooper smiles back through tight, crimson lips, and Nadja imagines her naked, in bed with Mr. Cooper. Angel in the throes of orgasm—is Angel capable of achieving orgasm? Yes, probably. Nadja is willing to concede that Angel, as cheerless as she appears to be in the office, is capable of relinquishing all and losing herself in the act.

Jerry clears his throat, smooths down his mustache, and the ceremony begins. He links his stunted lizard fingers and opens his mouth, inviting Mrs. Cooper to speak. Nadja glances at Mrs. Cooper, and gets stuck on Phil, who sits there, openly grimacing. Never mind that she is the one who trained him when he joined the firm. Maybe—Nadja tries to be charitable—he is uncomfortable, maybe even feeling sorry for her, and therefore the silly grimace.

Ah, the good old days when it was only the three of them in the room and she would sit and listen to Jerry and Phil exchange innuendoes and jokes. Now it is a different kind of joke, with Nadja blooming at the center of it.

There are many types of jokes in the universe. The joke she can now detach herself from and relegate to the soon-to-be-forgotten past is the joke of her sitting in a meeting with Jerry and Phil, supposedly discussing the all-important Information Project, when, out of God knows where, an image of their puny, damp penises would suddenly flash in her mind and, immediately following, an even more loathsome image, the image of her blowing them. The more Jerry and Phil disgusted her, the more frequent the images. This is how power was processed and transmogrified in her tortured employee brain. The only way to fight the images was to switch to the more realistic eventuality that she just might vomit her guts on Jerry's neat desk: bits of food in a dark torrent, directly from her stomach, would shower

Jerry and his desk. Depending on the angle, Phil, too, would get his share of the bounty. And what would she do? She would calmly march to the bathroom, her refuge, and rinse out her mouth. Job well done. Lose a few pounds and deluge the enemy in one go. Jerry would have to accept and swallow; you cannot fire a person for vomiting all over her boss's desk. It is nothing more, nothing less, than a gut reaction.

Where is she? In revenge land, of course. Mrs. Cooper has said her piece, and Jerry is suddenly talking and she is listening, but not exactly hearing him—a mental glitch. Nadja gazes at his moving lips, makes a concerted effort to pay attention; after all, he is talking about her future. She grasps something about cutbacks and corporate reorganization, but Jerry makes no mention of her many transgressions, including smoking pot in the bathroom one Friday afternoon to usher in the weekend. He does not have to: the text and protocol have been masticated in and regurgitated from the entrails of Human Resources, arriving readymade at a manager's desk. These days, any company worth its salt is streamlining, eliminating dregs.

Nadja concentrates on her Boss, trying to maintain a polite, affable expression. As Jerry speaks, she realizes that the title Boss may no longer apply, it is diminishing by the second, evaporating into thin air. It is actually expired, for Jerry, technically speaking, is no longer her Boss; he has released himself, has released them both, from this particular bond. But she is still required to sit there and listen. Or, is she? She could get up and say, Thank you, and walk out: tall, poised, and in control. What will they do? Run after her? Insist that she let them go through every stage of the performance so they can issue yet another detailed and useless report for their records?

She could leave, yes, but she remains rooted to the chair

by the last vestiges of obedience and curiosity. Yes, she has just been fired, goodbye and good luck. She thinks she detects a twitching muscle at the corner of Jerry's upper lip, right below his mustache, as if Jerry, while performing his employer-manager duty, is trying very hard to keep a straight face, as required during formal occasions and proceedings. It seems to Nadja that he wants to laugh, which makes her want to laugh, too. Finally, at the very end, she and Jerry will have reached some understanding, some common ground. Perhaps he, too, feels this tickle inside and is about to lose it, become hysterical—she and Jerry, the two of them set free, united in a seizure of mad hilarity. After all, he is only human. Considering everything, he was not all that bad. It is quite possible that he sincerely hoped they could be collegial. And yes, maybe she could have tried a little harder. All he ever wanted was a loyal employee he could trust—a perfectly understandable and legitimate expectation.

She becomes aware that on some level she is not even there, is not present in the room; her brain, as often happens, has taken off, following its own agenda, retreating to float where freedom and chaos intermingle.

Jerry is done speaking and it is Angel's turn again—a smooth transition, probably rehearsed, Nadja thinks. A pas de deux to be performed on the taut nerves of impudent employees. Angel is properly manicured and made-up, but her nose—the result of a bad nose job—is too small and narrow in her doughy face; Nadja imagines that Mrs. Cooper has trouble breathing through her remodeled nostrils.

The Angel of Death is as sweet as molasses and is strikingly articulate. She probably likes her job, laying people off, and she does it well. One day she may be called upon to lay herself off. Nadja concentrates on Angel's red mouth, her gleaming, pearly teeth. There seems to be such great coordinated harmony between Jerry and Angel, it is quite possible that the two of them make out on the side.

"Of course, we won't stand in the way of your collecting unemployment."

Unemployment! Nadja wakes up. "Stand in the way?"

"Contest it, which, as you know, we can."

They are not heartless, Mrs. Cooper asserts. Here, all Nadja need do is sign this form and that form, affirming she has no further claims, etc. etc., and they will grant her a generous compensation package. Not because they have to, but because they want to. They want to help her get back on her feet and find a job that suits her. And so, for once dutiful and willing, Nadja signs this form and that, and the ritual is over and done with. The magic words, "We wish you much success," have been uttered and she is free to go. Adios. Have a good life.

Her now stiff but always reliable legs carry her out of Jerry's office and back to her desk. She walks like a brand new robot, but, feeling that dignity is on her side, she remembers to straighten up her spine. Indeed, she is bristling with dignity and has no desire, nor the energy, to start packing. She has a sneaking feeling that people on the entire floor have heard the news and may be standing outside their cubicles, hoping to catch a glimpse of the drama's protagonist, maybe even allowing pity, rather than glee, into their hearts. She wants to call out: "Don't pity me, I'm fine, I'm happy to leave." But Angel, like bad air, hovers nearby.

Nadja turns to her. "Afraid I'll steal something, Mrs. Cooper?"

Angel smiles. "No, Nadja, regulations."

"Ah, regulations. What about decency?"

She is bristling again, this time with indignity. How dare they insult her like this, treat her as if she were a potential thief, or worse. She tells herself to cool it, but Angel bugs her, so smug and coy, empowered by the Firm to have the metaphorical last word. Maybe she should steal something, if only to warrant Mrs. Cooper's vigilance.

Nadja finds a shopping bag in a drawer and sets it on the chair. The truth is, there is not much she needs to pack. Except for a cardigan, a pair of sandals, and a couple of books, she has kept no personal items in the office. No framed photos, no plants, no cosmetics pouch. It is hard to believe that she spent nearly seven years of her life in this place: chair, desk, and misery. The funny-sad part: she will be replaced in no time. The next assigned victim will be thrilled, at least at first, to have her job. She will be thrilled to sit at this desolate post, gray and cold as a tombstone. The new employee may enliven her corner with photographs and a couple of small plants. The new employee may be a nicer, friendlier person than Nadja, an altogether more suitable employee, and, in the end, everyone will be happy for the change.

When Angel is momentarily distracted by the arrival of a security guard at the far end of the floor, Nadja cannot resist the opportunity and the temptation and slips a stapler into the shopping bag, burying it under the cardigan. For a moment she worries about being searched and getting caught, but it is too late: the stapler is in her bag. If she tries to return it to its rightful place, she will definitely be caught.

Angel escorts Nadja down the length of the hallway where she will entrust her into the good hands of the tall security guard, who will then shepherd her down the elevator and out to the street. On the way, Nadja stops to say goodbye to Betty, but Betty is clearly tense and awkward with Angel present, as if speaking to Nadja she is speaking to a traitor, a polluter.

"Where's Colleen?" Nadja asks in a soft voice to let Betty know she understands why Betty needs to act the way she does.

"She stepped away for a second," Betty says, then quickly adds, "we'll call you."

"Sure. Take care."

She is leaving the building for the very last time. A smiling Angel of Death, a hovering shadow, is behind Nadja, following her to the end of the hallway, where the security guard is waiting. Here, again, a smooth transfer of authority and guardianship until Nadja is safely outside their jurisdiction and is delivered to the public domain, belonging to no one and to everyone. Soon, Nadja and the security guard are in the elevator, enjoying a slow, quiet ride down twelve floors, the two of them staring up at the panel that flashes reassuringly: 11, 10, 9…

He is armed! Nadja realizes. She has never shared an elevator with an armed man before. She glances up at the dark, impassive face; she wants to believe he is a decent person with a boring, sometimes hateful, job.

She tries to make conversation. She sighs. "Well, who would have thunk. Just like that. They barely give you a chance to pack."

The guard offers no answer, except for a slight nod of the head, which she may have imagined.

"And this after seven years of hard labor." Nadja is determined to get a response out of him, even if it is just a chortle. "One day you're a loyal employee, the next you're worse than a leper."

4, 3, 2, L.

"Ain't that the truth," his response finally comes. In a nice, deep voice.

It is three o'clock in the afternoon and she is out on the street, a new person, an unemployed one, unfit and an eyesore in a corporate setting. Released into confusion and daylight. All around her, people are rushing from here to there. As usual. Only she among them can take her time and walk slowly, look here, look there. She is on holiday, on a furlough of indeterminate duration.

This is the first time she has been discarded like this, with so much pomp, with an Angel of Death standing by while she packs her things, and a security guard as companion on her Via Dolorosa, seeing her out of the building. A security guard who, like everyone else, was only doing his job—reluctantly, she was happy to note.

How many times has she fantasized about leaving this building never to return?

Beware what you wish for?

No, it is the right thing for her to be out of there, for her to be rid of them, and for them to be rid of her. She is a bit shaken, that's all, possibly in shock. She never imagined that they would dare fire her. After all, she did do her job, and a bit extra on the side. Just like the rest of them.

Well, they did, they did fire her, from her first real job. A job she did not like but stuck to it if only because it wasn't worse than the ones before it.

Yes, fired, discharged, and she had to sit there while two bureaucrats amused themselves, sadistically prolonging her ordeal, drawing satisfaction from the fact that even as she was being fired, they still held her in their power, the threat of denying her unemployment in the air. For, like Jerry implied, they could easily prove she was fired for good cause.

So, yes, she is a bit shaken, but also, on some level, she must be happy, no?

Well, not quite, not yet. Overwhelmed, yes. She has yet to adjust to her new situation.

She will go into a bar and sit for a while, she could use a drink. It may be too early for alcohol, but this is a special day, with special needs: she must sit down and recollect herself, calm her spirit, have a smoke.

On the immediate and very plus side: she did not have to wait until the gong in the sky struck five, allowing all the slaves, mostly females, to make a dash for the doors and elevators.

She enters a dim, cool bar, still empty of customers. She pulls a stool in the corner and orders a mug of beer. Soon, drawing on a cigarette and sipping her beer, she feels pleasantly woozy in the head. The bartender keeps busy, wiping, re-arranging glasses and bottles. Nadja has the feeling that he is uneasy, maybe self-conscious, with just one customer, and a female at that. She, too, in fact, feels a bit self-conscious, a bit out of place. Jerry and Angel, she imagines, are still in Jerry's office, rehashing the ceremony and discussing her, the bum, the loiterer, the outcast. If they saw her here, in the bar, drinking so early in the afternoon, all their suspicions would be substantiated, and therefore, as far as they are concerned, she has been duly declared obsolete, like some faulty piece of equipment. How superior they must feel, having had the upper hand, showing her the door. They pointed the finger at her and said, "Out!" banishing her from their small Garden of Eden.

A wave of self-pity and self-destruction washes over her. She burns with renewed humiliation for having sat and endured as Jerry and Angel serenaded each other past her. Then Angel, like a hawk, watching over her, as if she were a petty criminal, as if seven years of servitude counted for nothing. Good old Thoreau saw it right.

Secretly, she wipes tears from under her sunglasses. She sees herself jobless, Raoul-less, unable to pay the rent. Forever unpublished, forever toiling in vain. Having wasted her life, she is dying alone in some hovel.

She orders another beer, lights another cigarette.

The bartender, wiping a glass to a shine, turns to her. "Monday blues, huh?" he asks, good-humoredly.

She nods, smiles. "Worse than usual, yes." She hesitates; it is not her style to confide in strangers. "I just got fired."

"Oh." She senses that the bartender, the fatherly type, takes it to heart.

"Here," he says, placing a bowl of pretzels before her and, absurdly, this gesture elicits new tears from her eyes; Nadja pretends to look for something in her bag, and then in the shopping bag at her feet. Hidden from him, she wipes more tears.

"I wouldn't worry if I were you," he continues when she reappears from under. "You will soon find another job, and a better one, too. I'm sure of it."

"Oh yes, I know." She puts on a brave face and reaches for a pretzel. She chews, but cannot swallow; it dries out her mouth. She would like a glass of water, but does not want to trouble him with a service request; she washes down the pretzel with beer.

"There's always work for those who want it," says the bartender.

"True." In fact, she could work as a bartender, which is not a bad idea, and, it does not take much. She will attend bartender school for a couple of months, she will change her life, work a few hours every day in a bar, and then work on Woman late at night when everything around her is dark and quiet, her desk illumined by a small lamp.

She begins to feel rather gay and reassured. She quickly does the math and figures she can survive on $1,000 a month. Plus $200 for health insurance. Plus $100 for odds and ends. Grand total: $1,300. With unemployment and her savings and compensation package, she could survive for quite some time without a job. She may temp if she wants to, but only once in a while, if only to prove to herself she is still employable.

Before leaving, she prepares to pay for her beers, but the bartender will not hear of it. "My treat," he says. Timidly, she offers a tip, and he, with a smile and a shake of the head, waves it away.

Tears sting in her nostrils, and she stands there a moment, feeling contrite, undeserving. She must tell the bartender it was all her doing, she brought this on herself, he need not feel sympathy for her.

But all she can do is smile bashfully and head for the door. "Thank you," she remembers to say.

"Take it easy now," he calls after her, and she waves and is out the door.

She takes a few steps and stops. A new worry assaults her: the bartender may now be thinking she is a fake: she told him a story to get free beers from him. She must go back inside and insist on paying.

But how absurd she is! If she goes back inside, she will only confuse matters more, possibly hurting the bartender's feelings.

And why did she have to steal the stapler? She already has one at home. How many does she need?

Maybe she is just a little tipsy and a little overwrought. It is a good omen that the first person she met at the very start of her new life was a nice one. One day, she resolves, she will come back and thank him properly, presenting him with a gift. Maybe even her just-published book!

Now her step is quick and light, the step of a free person. In fact, just watching the people walking with her on the street makes her feel good, makes her feel she is part of life. Usually, when she feels sad, just walking outside and seeing people, puts everything in perspective.

Finally home, she takes a long shower, where she allows herself to shed more tears, possibly of relief. Oh, the way Jerry and Angel smiled at one another, complemented one another, always in perfect sync; in truth, a beautiful, if depraved, duet, a symphony, really, an opus!—Nadja snickers and howls into the stream of hot and soothing water. And all for the benefit of a stubborn child who would not listen while her corporate foster parents and benefactors want nothing better than to impart their hard-earned wisdoms.

Corporations, Raoul has told her, don't love you back. Corporations, she tells herself, are dictatorships comprised of many low-level tyrants.

At the kitchen counter she devours a sandwich and, beer in hand, she leaves the kitchen and gets on the phone, calling friends and describing the scene of her last employee hour. Later, she turns on the TV and tries to watch the news, but finds she has no patience to listen to the noise and chatter.

And so, somehow or other, it is past ten o'clock, and Nadja, wishing to prolong her wallowing in mild existential gloom, goes out for a walk. She thinks of Colette who said you must look for a long time at what pleases you, and even longer at what pains you, and her soul agrees—indeed! The night air is balmy, if a little muggy, and she feels like she could walk all night. She reminds herself that she no longer has to get up and rush to an office in the morning. No more zigzagging feet underground. No more hiding and lying. And: she is free to linger and doze on her pillow for as long as she wants. Nonetheless, she will rise early and set a new work routine. Including a daily run in the park. Every morning. Without fail!

There is a lot of human traffic in her neighborhood, and colors, and sounds. A man in front of her suddenly yells at someone across the street: "Do you see any other women pissing on the street?" but when she stops and looks to see who he is yelling at, she realizes he is yelling at no one in particular. The man continues to walk, and she does, too, keeping a safe distance from him. She thinks of Raoul who comforted her on the phone but could not come over. As it is, Raoul is missing out on a large chunk of her life, and maybe this is why she harbors a grudge against him, even though it is not his fault. Right now, she would have liked to walk hand in hand with a lover, maybe walk into a club and listen to jazz, and, if they felt like it, get a bite to eat. The city is full of possibilities, and yet her life is narrow.

Or, maybe not so narrow. There is something to be said for walking alone, a little tipsy, a romantic solitaire prowling the streets at night. Maybe she prefers this to gazing into someone's eyes, shutting out all the rest. Street people, mostly men, talk to her, not even asking for money, and she usually responds with a "Thank you," if they pay her a compliment. She would like to say more, maybe even stop and exchange a few words, but, at the same time, she also fears that her intentions would be misconstrued. The fact that they address her so readily, makes her think that she must look like them, or, at the very least, that they consider her to be one of them, a street person, a person of the night.

In a small Italian restaurant on East Houston, Raoul, ceremoniously, hands over the first installment: a $500 check. It feels a little awkward taking it from him, and yet, it feels right: now Raoul, too, has a stake in her future.

She smiles. "Did your hand tremble when you wrote out the check?"

"No." Raoul is emphatic. "I'm glad I can help. Especially now. It did feel strange, though, writing your name on a check, like a business expense."

"I am, in a way, a business expense."

"You're petty cash," Raoul says and they explode.

"Do you think it will change our relationship?" Nadja asks.

"Giving you money?" Raoul shrugs. "I don't think so. I hope not. Not on my end."

At the next table, an old lady with a cane rises from her table. The owner rushes to her side, inquiring about her health. "Thank God, still walking on my own three legs," the woman says, and Nadja smiles, looking at the woman and admiring her spirit in the face of debility and death.

Back home, she puts on *La Bohème* for Raoul to dance to. Sprawled on the couch, she watches his long skinny legs, his stocking feet, as he flits across the room like a ballerina clad in an undershirt. At times, when they dance together, she imagines that she suddenly has a heart attack, and she wonders whether Raoul will call for help, or will quietly sneak out.

She gets up to dance, watching her reflection in the window pane. Raoul, his eyes shut, now stands, his ear affixed to the loudspeaker, his arms and torso swinging like a great ape's. Nadja feels affection for the ape. She goes over to him and falls into his arms, and they dance together, mouth to mouth.

adja's next-door neighbor, Vivian, has just arrived home from work. She can hear Vivian unlock her door, she can hear Vivian's dog barking. It is a ritual they perform every evening in the hallway: the dog leaps out to greet his mistress, and she speaks to him in a happy, soothing voice: "Hello sweetheart, mommy's home, may I come in? Yes, sweetie, mommy's home." Now, in a low, seductive voice: "That's right, that's right. Are you happy to see your mommy? Good boy, good boy."

The dog is beside himself with joy, whimpering, almost wailing, his tail thumping Nadja's door. Nadja is a bit annoyed that the dog is thumping her door, but it would be absurd of her to go out there and complain. The poor dog is not to blame, he does not know it is Nadja's door, and, after a long day alone, no wonder he is so ecstatic, welcoming his mistress who will now feed him and take him for a walk. Nadja feels for the dog, locked up all day in a small apartment. It is a wasted life, she reflects, the life of city dogs: they turn stupid indoors. A whole society kept between walls, except for itinerary walks. She sees them often enough, out on the street, dogs and masters bound by a leash. When Nadja hears a master yell at his dog, she wants to say something sharp to the master, the same as when she hears an adult yell at a child. Of course, she keeps her mouth shut, but she feels her face and every muscle in her body tighten as she listens to the yelling and thinks of the abuse and humiliation the weak must accept as a fact of life. The other day, waiting at a street light, she noticed a skinny guy with his skinny dog at her side. These two, at least visually, seemed to belong together, but the guy was mean. "Sit!" he barked at the dog in a stern voice, and the dog, after a split-second of bewilderment, sat. Nadja wondered why it was so important to the guy that the dog sit, why he would not let the dog decide for itself if it wanted to sit or to stand while waiting for the light. A moment later the light changed, and the guy said: "Okay, let's go," and they went.

Every so often Nadja considers getting a pet, maybe a cat, maybe a turtle, but, so far, it has remained a passing thought, if only because she cannot imagine caring for a living thing. Years ago, she had a goldfish, magnificently alone in its tank. It was a beautiful fish with a long, delicate tail, and it lived with her for three years or so until the morning she woke up to the radio broadcast that Brezhnev had died. When she got up to feed the fish, it was nowhere in the tank. Frantically, she looked for it and found it behind the bookshelf, all dried up and shriveled, and it made her sick to imagine its last moments, gasping, trying to lift off the floor. For six months afterward, fish appeared in her dreams, fish jumping out of the tank as she tried to catch them with her bare hands to put them back in the water, all the while trying to cajole them with words, begging them to help her in her effort to save them. She still has the tank, now filled with rocks and pebbles, as well as a colorful marble she found on the street, and a small dusty American flag. When people ask why there are no fish in the tank, she says that the fish that used to live in the tank committed suicide the day Brezhnev died, and that she cannot bear the thought of having another.

Vivian's door is pulled shut, and quiet is restored. As Nadja rubs garlic over a slice of seeded rye toast—a delicacy—she thinks of love lavishly bestowed on the dog next door. On the evening news: bombs explode in various parts of the globe. Planes fall out of the sky, the fuselage dug out from ocean floors. Horror-inducing details about sharks and body parts; the newscasters, in their slick, all-important way, are avidly and graphically specific.

Nadja wants to tear herself away from couch and the TV, but is too lethargic.

The telephone startles her. She mutes the TV and talks to Sabine who is lonely in her cottage by the sea and is getting old with Butterscotch in her lap.

"All I need now," Sabine says, "is a rocking chair."

Nadja laughs.

"I was thinking, since Butterscotch is in my lap, it is only me who is getting old. Does it make any sense? Like, relativity, you know? And, if it's only me who's getting old, then Butterscotch will not have to die. You have no idea how much I worry about him."

"Don't worry about Butterscotch," Nadja says. "He'll outlive you."

"Thanks, Nadja. Are you saying I'm going to die soon? Am I going insane?"

"Why don't you come to the city for a few days? You may find a lover, or someone to play with for a few salacious hours."

"No." Sabine lets out a sigh. "I love my house. Remember the contractor I told you about? Well, he has the nerve to knock on my door this morning…"

Nadja listens. It requires little effort, and at this late hour it is almost a comfort to listen to Sabine's endless stream. Sabine will often repeat the same stories, or themes, but the stories never lose their urgency and the ardor of the aggrieved. She may be complaining about a lover who ditched her yesterday, or twenty years ago, it makes no difference, for both stories, and the hurt, still burn vividly in Sabine's brain.

And her parents, too, she says. They always left her behind, their only child, never taking her with them when they went on vacation. And at the dinner table, they never included her in their conversation and never bothered to listen to her. And all these other people she knows, they all talk down to her, and she cannot understand why. Why are they so mean? True, she is not an angel, but she tries to be fair. Maybe it is not people, Nadja suggests. Maybe it is lovers you can't get along with. No, no, Sabine insists, it is not just lovers, but people in general. They ignore and avoid her, they won't invite her to dinner. Why won't they invite you to dinner? Do you invite them? Nadja asks. No, Sabine admits, but she is single right now, separated from Diane, so why won't this dyke couple she knows invite her over and introduce her to people. They've been on the island much longer than she, they know people. Couples should take care of singles, it's only fair. This couple could introduce her to the other women on the island, but the entire dyke community shuns her.

Soon, Nadja is thinking, she will go to bed. She will read for a while and fall asleep. Receiver nestled between ear and shoulder, she concludes yet again that another day is over. No one is happy.

"Why don't you come out this weekend? All you need do is get yourself on the jitney. I'll pay your fare if you can't afford it. Both ways!"

"Both ways—how grand of you!" Nadja reciprocates. She considers the offer and decides that yes, it will do her good to get away for a couple of days. "Great," she says, "I'll come, but I'll pay my own way, I'm not destitute, yet. Do you need something from the city?" Nadja adds, dreading the answer.

"No, just come."

On the jitney, Nadja reads and rereads a poem by Gwendolyn Brooks, "The Lovers of the Poor," about the Ladies from the Ladies' Betterment League who give money to the poor, but only to the worthy poor, "The very very worthy/And beautiful poor. Perhaps just not too swarthy?/Perhaps just not too dirty nor too dim/Nor—passionate." Once in while she looks up and out the window, or furtively observes her fellow-passengers. She does not really belong among these well-to-do, well-dressed persons, traveling to the shore as a matter of course. In the seat in front of her, a woman daintily bites into a bagel and cream-cheese sandwich—so fresh and crisp and appetizing. Nadja imagines the woman's pleasure as her teeth make contact with the crust, as her tongue and saliva are set in motion and every fiber of her being is enmeshed in the delight of chewing and swallowing. If Nadja had a bagel and cheese, she would prolong the feast for as long as possible.

Nadja wets her lips. She was not hungry before, but now she is. She should have brought a sandwich, or an apple. Ah, well, she did not think of it. Hopefully, Sabine will have a late lunch all laid out for them on the porch.

At the station, she is surprised to find that Sabine is already there, forlorn behind the wheel even though her tush is cushioned in leather. Nadja feels herself smile and, mindful of the oncoming traffic, she quickly crosses the street and gets in the car.

In her seat, Nadja leans over toward Sabine—kiss, kiss.

"Did you miss me?" Nadja asks.

"Desperately," Sabine says, and Nadja laughs.

As they drive to the cottage, Sabine, in a monotone, tells Nadja about plumbers, carpenters, gardeners, and Nadja tries to listen, while watching the landscape rushing past, the occasional vineyard, the fruit and vegetable stands, the plants nurseries. She imagines living out here year-round, quietly, dwelling in a small house, with a small husband and kids.

"So, what should I do?" Sabine asks.

"About what?"

"Aren't you listening?"

"I am. I missed the last part."

"My floors. Should I sand them this year or next?"

"Hmmm. Next year."

Nadja unpacks, then sits on the porch with a beer and a cigarette, contemplating the water; Sabine is inside, making lunch. The sky is overcast, and the water is a bit agitated, but swimmable. Soon, Sabine comes out and they sit down to a delicious lunch of tuna-salad sandwiches.

"I'm famished!" Nadja's hand trembles as she reaches for a sandwich.

"Eat, my dear, eat," Sabine says. "You know, I've been thinking." Sabine bites into her sandwich. "I really think it is a good thing that they fired you. It's time you took a couple of years off to devote yourself fulltime to your writing career."

"I don't think of writing as a career, but you're right, it'll be good for me to write fulltime."

"Better change your attitude. Writing is a career. You have to put yourself out there, be aggressive. Publishers spend money to make room for you on the market, they expect to see a return on their investment, otherwise you're worthless to them. They want to see a persona, someone who's talk-show compatible. Anyway, if you need cash, I'll help you."

Nadja looks at Sabine, at her singular straight nose, her singular, grayish-foxy eyes, her singularly pale, thin lips. It is a singularly, asymmetrically, attractive face.

"You know what I think?" Nadja says. "I think that if worse comes to worst I'll just move in with you, become a dyke or a maid."

"You're not my type, sweetie. Maybe my slave."

Later the sky clears, and they go in for a long swim. They hover on their stomachs and watch the small fishes frolic below; once in a while, a crab hurries along. They come out of the water and lie down on the warm sand; before long, they shut their eyes and drift into sleep. When they wake, they watch the sun disappear below the horizon, and then take turns under the hot stream of water in the outdoor shower. Nadja says she loves the outdoor shower, it is the best feature of the cottage, and Sabine recommends that Nadja use the liquid baby soap from Origins that makes the skin feel smooth and fragrant. Nadja observes Sabine—stocky and muscular, her breasts small and so perfectly round and firm, they look manmade. Nadja delights in the baby soap, reflecting that she does not feel self-conscious with Sabine in the shower, as she would with Deirdre, or with other female friends. She and Sabine are like two little girls, trapped in women's bodies.

Wrapped in large towels, they collapse onto the lounge chairs on the beach, facing the water. Nadja, without wanting to, is thinking about home, seeing herself sitting at her desk.

"How do you feel?" Sabine asks.

"Good," Nadja says dreamily. "But I'm still getting used to the idea that I'm free, absolutely free. There's this jumble in my head, it could be fear."

"You can always get another job."

"I don't think I'd want to, not after a prolonged period of freedom."

"How will you manage?"

"You'll support me. Only kidding. Maybe I'll temp. Maybe… I don't know, we'll see."

"I'll probably be stuck with you for the rest of my life," Sabine says, and they crack up.

It is getting dark. A few stars appear in the sky and, across the water, lights twinkle as people in Connecticut prepare for dinner. Soon, she and Sabine will do the same. Nadja feels mellow, in peace with herself and her surroundings. She leans back in the chair and shuts her eyes. What a day.

"It's so nice and quiet here," she says after a while. "You're lucky you don't have noisy neighbors."

"Uh-huh."

"Are you falling asleep again?"

"No. Are you?"

"No. just mellowing. We're both so nice and mellow."

"Nice, I don't know. Mellow, maybe." Sabine lets out a sigh. "I'm thinking what to do about dinner. I can make my special vegetable casserole."

"Sounds good. I can make my special rice."

"What's your special rice?"

"Rice with a spoonful of shredded coconut."

"Hmmm. We don't have shredded coconut."

"Too bad. Just rice, then, and maybe a few raisins and chopped almonds?"

"All right."

"You know," Nadja says with a new awareness. "I think I'm changing. I think I can feel it."

"Changing how?" Sabine sits up in her chair, and so does Nadja.

"Just changing. My whole character is changing. Not having

to leave the house in the morning has done something to my psyche."

"I hope not," Sabine says. "You'll become arrogant and impossible to deal with."

"Just the opposite, my dear. I'll become a much nicer person, no longer as harassed and pressed for time as I used to be. I may even reach the stage where I won't mind spending hours on the phone, listening to you."

"That would be nice. I can fire my shrink!"

"By the way." Nadja remembers. "I meant to ask you. When we're naked, in the shower let's say, are you, like, uncomfortable?"

"Why should I be uncomfortable?"

"Because, you know, a naked female body?"

"Oh, Nadja," Sabine's voice rises. "It kills me how straight women have this absurd notion that they're irresistible, that if a lesb lays her eyes on one, she immediately desires her."

"No need to get so excited." Nadja is amused. "All I'm saying is, if I were to take a shower with a man, even one who is absolutely not my type, I'd still be, you know, not aroused exactly, but there would be something, a tickle maybe?"

"Really? Why?"

"Why?! Because there's always this tension between men and women, I'm sure you must know this?"

"No, I don't. Not really," Sabine says in a low voice. "I never felt it, not a sexual tension. Frankly, the whole business is puzzling to me. I, for one, don't quite believe that women are truly aroused by men. They've been conditioned to believe that they need a man for their physical and emotional and, of course, financial security and well-being. The fact of the matter is, seventy percent of women in this country don't achieve orgasm with men, which, of course, earns them the frigid label. You, of the famed orgasms, being an exception, of course."

Nadja laughs. "It's so nice when it's just the two of us. When there's a third person around, you become impossible."

"I know," Sabine say. "My competitive side acts up. Which reminds me. Karen and Edgar are coming tomorrow to spend the afternoon and maybe stay for dinner. You don't know them, but I think you will like them."

"All right."

Sabine pushes up from the chair. "Are you hungry?"

"I could eat."

"Let's," Sabine says and they go up the path and into the house.

All night, Nadja tosses and turns on the narrow sofa in the living room—the guest room is shut for renovations. Thoughts and images come at her with great velocity from every file and folder in her brain, and the constant roar of the water pounds in her ears and heart. Finally, at five in the morning, she gives up on sleep. She makes coffee, feeds Butterscotch, and goes down to the beach. A hint of light illumines the sky but it is still dark, and the rush of the waves is loud and angry. She hugs herself against the wind, against the menace of chaos and destruction this gray and choppy waterscape suggests. In childhood nightmares, a wall of water advanced on shore, sweeping everything; this was long before she had ever heard the term tsunami. She sticks her tongue out to lick the fine spray, and shouts against the roar: "You are magnificent."

More light spreads in the sky. Butterscotch roams the dunes, and Nadja jogs barefoot on the wet sand, past sleepy beachfront cottages, rising up from the sand in various geometrical shapes.

When she is done jogging, she does her stretching exercises, then turns around and bends over to look at the water from between her knees. It is an upside-down view, and it takes her a moment to adjust and figure out what she sees. Everything is reversed: the foamy waves still rush to shore, yet seem to recede from her. It is like watching a person talking from an upside down view as the top lip becomes the bottom lip, and the teeth, incongruently, do a different, denture- ike number.

A couple of hours later, they go out for a power walk. Nadja stands and watches as Sabine pulls on her socks in an ultimately efficient yet seemingly haphazard manner. Then the sneakers: a swift, expert tying of the laces with minimal wrist movement. Sabine, Nadja thinks, is a peculiar blend of scattered confusion and shrewd precision. Nadja often wonders about Sabine's brain, about how it works. In some ways, she and Sabine are alike, and yet they are worlds apart. Humans, she reflects, are inscrutable. Like newborn babies and cats.

They walk uphill. It is windy, but the sky is clear blue. Nadja glances at Sabine; she seems downcast. "Do you wake up depressed?" Nadja asks.

Sabine shrugs. "Mostly I'm just too exhausted to feel anything."

"We're so spoiled," Nadja says. "My parents, who had a much harder life, never complained. I don't know how they managed it."

"We are spoiled. I'm sorry I never got to meet your parents."

"I know. They either died too soon, or I met you too late."

"Can't it be both?" Sabine asks in all sincerity and Nadja laughs. Right this minute, she loves Sabine.

In the late afternoon, the winds abate, and Karen and Edgar, a husband-and-wife team, arrive. The four of them recline on a blanket on the beach, drinking beer and munching on seaweed potato chips. Nadja is the only smoker—yet another ingredient that sets her apart as Sabine and her guests serenely exchange reviews and opinions about the service and the quality of food in upscale restaurants in the city—a sanctioned pastime as well as an exercise in status assertion and assessment of the other. Thanks to Raoul, Nadja, too, is somewhat conversant on such topics, and she pretends to be as casual and carefree as they seem to be, even if she feels fraudulent and silly engaging in this game. She can sense that Sabine is glad and relieved that Nadja can participate, and so be approved, at least initially, by her friends.

Periodically, in flashes, Nadja recalls her still fresh and new situation. She has yet to adjust to this total freedom, this total dependence on the self. She does not goof off, she is diligent at her desk everyday, and no paycheck accompanies her efforts. Those who do not get paid for their time are considered losers, unless they are millionaires, in which case it does not matter what they do or do not do with their time.

Briefly, she feels a bitterness toward the three seated around her, for whom money is an abstraction. And yet, she concedes, envy is the engine that drives the bitterness she feels.

Husband Edgar says they dined at Nobu the other night. They were not impressed, he is sorry to report. He and wife Karen do not understand what the hype is all about.

"Really?" Sabine's face lights up with astonishment and maybe also with glee, and Nadja cannot tell whether Sabine is genuinely astonished, or is simply glad for the opportunity to suggest that her tastes are finer. "I've eaten there a couple of times and thought it was fabulous."

Ignoring Sabine's remark, Karen turns to Nadja. "Have you eaten there?" she asks.

"Not yet," Nadja admits. She and Raoul have discussed going there, but decided it was a bit too ostentatious for them.

"I love their tasting menu," Sabine says.

"They're overpriced," Karen says. "I can't see paying so much for sushi."

"It's more than just sushi." Sabine is adamant.

"Call it what you like, it's still raw fish." Karen smiles.

"You're paying for the hype and the decor," Edgar puts in. "It's a scam."

"It's not a scam," Sabine almost screams, as she always does when she feels outnumbered or out-argued. "You always pay for the decor when you go to these places. You're just being snobbish in your own misguided way."

"Please, let us not argue." Karen has a soft voice and she speaks very slowly. Nadja can imagine her speaking this way to a child, possibly driving the child nuts. But Karen and Edgar do not have children, and are more or less past the age.

"These potato chips are delicious," Edgar says.

"Yes!" They all agree.

Surreptitiously, Nadja studies Karen and Edgar, trying to see what makes them a couple. She is looking for a sign of affection, for some connection between them. She observes Karen's long fingers, the very pale skin, faintly bluish with veins.

Sabine, sifting sand, begins to discuss the stock market with Edgar. She recommends that he buy a certain stock, when Karen interjects. "We're broke," she says coolly, even proudly.

How can they be broke and dine at Nobu? Nadja wonders. But then, moneyed people, as a rule, are always broke. It is mystifying to Nadja why they would even say such a thing, and yet, she concludes, they must believe they are truly broke. She, who in reality could be considered broke, never declares herself broke, never thinks of herself as broke. Of course, her bills and theirs do not compare, so, relatively speaking, they may very well be broke. Sabine, too, often complains about being broke, and then goes out on a shopping spree. These three would be horrified were she to tell them she plans to subsist, and quite honorably, on $1,300 a month.

She looks out to the water, pondering the depths of shrewd minds, cold hearts. She recalls the Brooks poem she has read on the Jitney and tries to imagine how these three would react were she to read the poem to them. She doubts they give money to the worthy poor, let alone a dirty beggar on the street. She wonders what friendship means in cutthroat circles where the stakes, potentially, are much higher. She imagines they must have different codes of behavior, harboring no illusions of harmony and good will between people. They are probably more matter-of-fact, ruthlessly detached and uncaring about others, allowing no room for sentiments and weakness. And yet, what does she know? She is not one of them, she is not in their shoes.

"Excuse me," she says and stands up. She leaves them on the sand and goes into the house. Butterscotch, dozing on a chair, looks up, and Nadja has the uncomfortable feeling that even the cat knows that she does not belong. All at once, she has a vision of herself, a few years from now, a modern-day spinster, a failure in every respect, living in the same small apartment, in the same dilapidated building, temping for a living.

She grabs a pen and sits down at the table to figure out her finances once again. She likes playing with numbers, especially when she can make them work in her favor. She has done this sort of calculation so many times in the past, she has it down to a science. Yes, $1,300 a month. Her unemployment checks should begin arriving soon, and, with her savings and Raoul's donations, she should be able to survive without a job for about two or three years, maybe even a little longer.

Now calm, even content, she goes into the bathroom and, as she flushes the toilet, she amuses herself with the thought that she leaves her droppings in other people's homes. It's a strange feeling, actually, leaving something so private and yet generic. Pensive, she goes out to the porch and looks at the three huddled on the blanket; they seem so small and guileless against the blue vastness and the bright red sun that has begun its descent.

"Can I get you anything?" she calls.

"No," Sabine calls back. "We'll have dinner soon."

Over lobster dinner, Sabine tells her guests that Nadja has joined the ranks of the unemployed, having been fired from her job. This elicits mild interest from Karen and Edgar.

"Why did they fire you?" Karen asks.

Nadja shrugs. "I'm not sure," she says, and Karen nods as she cracks the lobster's shell, her very white fingers now oily and shiny. Waiting to see if Karen will lick her fingers clean, Nadja wonders if Karen is still interested in her story and if she should go on with the telling, but Karen, right now, seems to be concentrating on the task at hand, fishing with her fork for a piece of meat still hiding in a claw. "I think," Nadja continues anyway, "it was simply the fact that my boss couldn't stand me, I was an affront to his ego. And they caught on to the fact that I was doing other work."

"No kidding." Edgar looks up from his plate. "They actually caught you?"

Nadja observes the sprouting hairs on Edgar's fingers and his quite long fingernails. He is wearing a thick, assertive wedding band. Raoul does not wear a band. Raoul bites his nails down to the cuticle, a trait Nadja fondly treasures: no unwanted scratches in delicate parts. She makes a mental note to remember to ask Sabine about lesbians and nails. "They found a page in the Xerox machine."

"What do you mean?" Karen asks.

"She was working on her novel in the office," a smirking Sabine elucidates.

"Weren't you afraid that they would catch you?" Karen asks.

"I was careful," Nadja says. "The other option would have been to die of boredom at my desk. Most employees, by the way, engage in some outside activity at the office. Einstein did it, too, but he was never caught."

"How do you know?" Edgar asks.

"I'm reading a biography of him. And, later in life, when he lived in Princeton, he could be seen picking cigarette butts off the street."

"Comparing yourself to Einstein?" Sabine mocks.

"Mind you," Nadja addresses Sabine, "he, too, wanted to know why the sky is blue. The only difference between him and me, he figured it out."

"Very funny." Sabine pauses. "Well, are you going to let us in on the secret, or are you going to keep us in suspense?"

"He says that dust and air molecules reflect the blue part of light more so than the rest of the spectrum."

"I kind of knew that," Sabine says.

"Of course."

Edgar is pensive. "Was your name on it, on the page they found?"

"No."

"Then they have no proof. You can sue them, you know?" Edgar is a lawyer.

"Not really," Nadja says. "I don't have the energy, and they gave me a generous enough compensation package. Besides, they had other grievances against me, all of them absolutely true."

"Well, that's another matter. What else did they have?"

"My general attitude, I guess. And smoking pot in the bathroom."

Now they all respond together. Edgar gasps, "You smoked pot?" Sabine sort of giggles, crying, "You what?" and Karen smiles and says, "Cool."

"But only once, on a Friday afternoon," Nadja adds with a small, self-contented smile.

"You never told me this. How did they know it was you?" Sabine asks.

"They didn't, but they needed a suspect and, as usual, I was it."

"Listen to this," Sabine takes over. "After she is fired, she goes into this bar to get drunk, and the bartender won't let her pay for her drinks."

"I didn't get drunk."

"Why won't he let her pay?" Edgar asks.

"Isn't it obvious?" Sabine says. "He felt sorry for her. Seeking sympathy, she told him she just got fired."

Karen, wiping her hands on her napkin, leans toward Nadja. "What are you going to do now?"

Nadja tries to sound nonchalant. "I think I'll be all right. I'm still on the payroll for three months, I'm collecting unemployment, and I have some savings."

"Will it be enough?"

"Her boyfriend gives her money," Sabine sees fit to announce.

"Oh," Karen says.

"Tax free," Sabine adds.

"Legally speaking," Edgar says, "it's taxable income. There's a certain amount you may consider a gift, but beyond that—"

"Edgar, please," Karen cuts him off.

"All right, all right."

"He can't help himself," Karen explains. "It is always figures and formulas, putting things in order."

"I just wanted Nadja to be aware of her situation."

"I'm sure Nadja knows enough to handle her own affairs."

Fascinated, Nadja watches Edgar and Karen, thinking of Lydia and Raoul.

"Actually, I wouldn't count on that," Sabine says.

A quick worried glance from Karen at Nadja.

"She's only kidding," Nadja assures Karen.

"I can never tell with Sabine." Karen leans her elbows on the table. "What a strange name, Sabine. Sounds like a witch's name."

"It's not strange at all, it's different," Sabine says, to which Edgar responds with a resounding, "Of course!" and Karen lets out a soft sound, maybe a laugh. Nadja experiences a spark of something akin to affection for Karen and Edgar.

"I must have done something awful in a previous life," Sabine says in a plaintive voice. "Why do I always get stuck with guests who abuse me after I've fed them?"

"Because you invite it." Karen laughs, patting Sabine's hand. "And because we love you."

"I wish it were true, I need people to love me."

"I often wonder," Edgar says, "if fundamentally that's all we really need, to have others love us."

The females at the table scrutinize the male.

"In other words, do we really want to be loved, or do we simply look for someone who would listen to us?" Edgar pauses, as if unsure he's got their attention. "Someone who would be sympathetic to our point of view? We have this unrelenting need to be heard, to be counted. We want someone we can tell our story to, someone who would understand and appreciate our wonderfulness."

There's a brief silence, soon broken by Sabine. "And that's exactly what you're doing right now, and quite successfully I might add. You're venting your need, usurping our attention in typical male fashion."

"Precisely my point," Edgar says.

"What is your point, Edgar?" Karen asks.

Edgar turns a focused gaze on his wife, but says nothing for a while. "Damn, I seem to have lost it," he says, now addressing Sabine, "thanks to you, Sabine. Anyway, I was trying to explain that love, the word love, is too broad and vague to convey anything. I was about to develop this idea, it made so much sense only a minute ago, and now it's gone, even though I still have it inside me, I still feel what I was going to tell you, but the overall structure, the words, are lost."

Nadja smiles, nodding.

"Isn't he cute?" Karen says. "He is sizzling tonight."

"Expensive wine will do that," Sabine says. "Who's driving, by the way?"

"I am," Karen says.

Sabine turns to Nadja. "They've just leased a Honda, just like mine, but I have leather seats! Isn't it amazing that we got the same car?"

"Very," Nadja says.

When the guests leave, Nadja and Sabine clear the table, then linger on the porch, dunking chocolate cookies in hot tea. The night air carries a bit of a chill, and Sabine gives Nadja one of her heavy pullovers.

"Did you like them?" Sabine asks.

"Well." Nadja tries to decide. "I don't really know them. There were moments when I liked them, superficially, I guess. On the whole, though, they seem to float. Especially Karen. Edgar is more down to earth, I think, maybe more adventurous. How about you? Do you like them?"

"I should hope so," Sabine says. "At least I think I do, most of the time. I've known them forever, I'm used to them, but I feel much closer to you. I feel I can be open and relaxed with you in a way I can't be with them."

"Hmmm. Maybe because they're a couple?"

"Not really. I'm close with Lucy and George. But maybe you're a better person? Someone I feel I can trust?"

"Thank you."

"I said, maybe. Anyway, when I first knew him, Edgar was gay. Then he met Karen and went straight, or so he says. This is strictly between you and me."

"Not to worry." Nadja leans back in her chair and rests her feet up on the table. She waits for Sabine to voice a complaint, but Sabine is quiet. "You know, now that I am without a job, maybe I should go into business. I have no trouble imagining myself as the proprietor of a small bagel shop, or a coffee specialty shop, catering to a select clientele, mostly friends who drop in for coffee and a chat. And since it's my own business, it's like being at home. I don't mind it at all having to go in every morning, taking care of my customers, my employees. And, at the end of each day, I feel in my bones the deep satisfaction of a laborer after a long day of good, honest work and, of course, another dollar in my pocket. I lock up, get on the train and go home, have dinner with the wife and kids."

"You mean, husband and kids," Sabine offers sleepily.

"No, I mean wife and kids. I'm always a man when I have this fantasy."

"Interesting." All at once, Sabine leaps forward in her chair, fully awake. "Don't you think it was weird the way Karen kept harping about my name?"

"She didn't, really."

"I love my name. I was named after my grandmother who had died in the camps."

"I know," Nadja says. She, too, had been named after a grandmother she never knew. "Fucking Germans," she adds softly, with no animosity; just saying and hearing the words has a soothing effect. Most people probably avoid reading books about the Holocaust, but Nadja is addicted, forever sickened and trying to come to terms with the fact that the organized slaughter went on for the many years that it did; forever presented with the possibility that it may be the faces of relatives she is looking at when watching documentaries where Jews, wearing the yellow star, are accosted on the street, or are hauled onto a train, or are pushed out of it upon arriving in a camp where they will be gassed and burned.

"My trainer at the gym is German," Sabine says. "I like him, though. He told me that Goebbels said in his diary that the Jew was a waste product."

"They were all thugs, beginning with the so-called elite of the Nazi regime. Mad dogs and Prussian proud."

"You know, I often have dreams about Nazis out to kill me."

"I used to have them, too," Nadja says slowly. It feels good to sit on the porch in the dark and let the conversation take them wherever it goes even if it has to do with Nazis and old, persistent pain. "I had one recurrent dream with the same basic plot where Nazis with guns are chasing me in the forest. I hated myself in the dream for being such a coward, running for my life, hiding behind a tree and trembling with fear."

"You were probably dreaming your parents' traumas," Sabine says. "My shrink says that we live out our parents' dark side."

"I don't know," Nadja says. "Maybe."

"Diane Arbus once said that since we live in a world where no one is spared human trauma, the deformed among us are the true aristocrats because they were born with theirs."

Nadja nods. "Arbus herself was one. She was Jewish, you know."

"Are you sure? I don't remember her being Jewish."

"She was. Her grandparents were Russian immigrants," Nadja says. "By the way, are they really broke? Edgar and Karen?"

"Who said they were broke?"

"She did."

"She was probably joking."

"No, I thought she meant it."

"Yeah, well, the way she meant it bears no relation to the way you heard it."

Nadja laughs. "I'm sure. You, too, complain that you're broke, and you go shopping. Maybe it's a fad, or a code of some kind?"

"What is?"

"Declaring yourself broke?"

Sabine gurgles, laughing through her nose. "Compared to them, I am a welfare case. He's a lawyer, she's a food designer. No kids, not even pets. They should adopt you, as a matter of fact."

"I could use a pair of young, dynamic, well-to-do parents. My parents had so much on their minds, making do in a new country, not to mention their nightmare of a past."

"Do you miss them?"

"What a question. Of course I miss them. I miss having parents."

"I can't bear the thought of my parents dying."

"You're lucky to have them both still living. What I regret most is that my parents never lived to see me become a person, make something of myself. I have this idea they were disappointed in me, although I'll never know for sure unless I become a parent myself, which, at this point, is quite unlikely."

"I don't think they were disappointed," Sabine offers meekly.

"Maybe not, but it kills me to think that I never saw them as people, but only as something that existed to take care of me. Kids by nature are little angelic monsters."

"True. That's why I don't think I'd want to have a child. Diane and I talked about adopting, but, of course, it doesn't look like it's going to happen."

"If I could impregnate a guy, I would definitely want a child. I'd be a real mensch, I'd be there for him during pregnancy and through labor. I'd hold his hand and lovingly stroke his stomach to feel the baby kick. I'd get up in the middle of the night, bring the baby to his tit so the baby can suckle—"

"Ugh, Nadja! What a revolting picture, a hairy chest."

"Baby gorillas happily suck on hairy chests."

"We're not gorillas."

"But our perceptions may evolve. A thousand years from now, who knows, men will take on the onus of birth."

"No way," Sabine says." Women will never give up the power of giving birth."

"I'm not so sure. Women are changing, and men are changing too. We're still evolving. And there are species in nature where the roles are reversed and the male is the one giving birth."

They are quiet for a while, looking out to the water. Stars of variously shining brightness are pinned up above, and small waves, in rhythmic intervals, break at the shore. The neighboring houses are dark and quiet.

"Wow," Nadja says. "It suddenly hits me again, and powerfully, the idea that I'm free. I don't have this thing hanging over my head."

"What thing?"

"This shadow. Of the office. Of course, you can't know what I'm talking about. You wouldn't last in an office for more than five minutes. You'd be fighting with everyone as soon as you walked in."

"Probably."

Sabine sounds tired. Soon, Nadja reflects, they, too, will turn out the lights and go to sleep, make the darkness complete. A breeze lifts from the water, goosebumping Nadja's skin; she thinks of autumn.

"Isn't it something?" Nadja says. "The seasons?"

"I love it out here," Sabine murmurs. "I don't even miss the city."

"The way the seasons change?"

"Are you being wistful?"

"Remember Burt Lancaster in "Atlantic City," when he points at the ocean and says, 'Ah, the Atlantic Ocean used to be something in those days'?"

"You know what my real life problem has always been? I'm afraid of the void. My shrink says I expend too much energy, trying to avoid the void. That's why I feel exhausted all the time, a kind of low-level anxiety. He says I masturbate so much not for physical pleasure but to avoid the void."

Nadja is shocked. "You tell him you masturbate?"

"Why not? I don't go into the details."

"Thank God," Nadja says, wondering what goes on in the shrink's mind as he sits there, listening to Sabine's masturbation tales. "Aren't you embarrassed to discuss it with him, with a man?"

"You don't understand therapy. You're supposed to talk about things. You don't fear the void, do you?"

Nadja takes a moment. "I think I do, but only in spurts, like everybody else."

"You think a plumber in Brooklyn fears the void?"

"I certainly don't believe that so-called artists and writers can claim a monopoly on anxiety and on fearing the void."

"Are you truly that fucking healthy, or do you just pretend?"

Nadja laughs, then decides to light a cigarette and takes just two puffs to end the night.

"Actually, your compulsion to work all the time is possibly your way of avoiding the void. I suppose now that you're out of a job, you're working from morning to night, like a true and dedicated obsessive?"

Nadja exhales white smoke against the sky. "A true monk, yes. But writing is a kind of abdication, and this is a direct quote, as you surely know."

"No, I don't." Sabine seems anxious for not knowing. "But I like it. Who said it?"

"Blaise Cendrars."

"Remind me again tomorrow, I want to look him up. Anyway, I used to write more when I was poor. My anxiety about money must have been greater than my anxiety about the void."

"You were never really poor, your parents are well-off."

"They didn't use to be. I told my shrink that you don't have a dark side, but he says that you do and that you hide it from people."

Nadja looks out to the water; it pulls like a magnet. The dark side again. As if it were a banner, something to hold up and brag about. Sabine makes her feel defensive for not "having it" or "hiding it."

"Your shrink never met me. How would he know what I have or what I'm hiding when you're the only source?"

"Good shrinks can extrapolate. They know about these things."

"Well," Nadja kills the cigarette and then continues, making it up as she goes. "If the dark side means the allure of danger, the desire to touch what lies beyond, then we all have it. It's called the id?"

"The question is, are you aware of it? Most people aren't aware of it."

"How do you know? Maybe they just don't talk about it."

"You know, Nadja, maybe I should just quit torturing myself and be like you? Simple-minded?"

"Well my dear Sabine, this is not such a bad idea. Then you and I, and presumably your shrink, may finally achieve some peace and quiet."

"Fat chance," Sabine mutters.

In the morning, after a quick swim, they are at the counter, making breakfast. Nadja is in an especially good mood as she listens to Sabine who is trying to figure out whether or not she misses Diane, and then decides that she doesn't miss her. She knows it's not fair, Sabine admits, but she does tend to mistreat her lovers. "I have this perverse need to treat them as furniture. I also need them to be cunning, conniving, preferably perverse," she says.

The exact opposite of me, Nadja reflects. Sabine thrives on drama and conflict, whereas she, if she can help it, avoids conflict.

"What about nails?" Nadja remembers. "Dykes and nails? Raoul bites his, and I was wondering—"

Sabine snorts. "That's a very obvious question."

"Is it?"

"Of course. Interesting, though, that you thought about this kind of problem." Sabine sucks air through her lips, then grudgingly divulges, "Dykes cut their nails. Like, when they meet someone and are about to have sex, they'll cut their nails."

"You mean, just before going to bed? Like you would go into the bathroom to put in your diaphragm?"

"Something like that. I'm very irritated that you thought of it."

"Why? You just said it was obvious."

"Well, it is to us," Sabine says smugly. "It's a secret of the trade."

"But it's a perfectly sensible thing to wonder about."

"Not for most people. The average person is not going around, thinking about dykes."

"But it's not just a dyke problem, it's every woman's problem, and a problem for guys too." Nadja takes Sabine's hand. "Your nails are pretty long."

"My misfortune, yes. Telltale sign I haven't had sex in a while." Sabine contemplates her nails. "I usually keep them fairly short." She sighs. "Oh, Nadja, I need to get laid, badly. I've been feeling this incredible need to shove something into my body, some body part, preferably a hand."

Nadja laughs, mystified by, and somewhat envious of, Sabine's insatiable needs. "Don't lose heart, dear, the right part will come."

"Very amusing. I can't stand it that you're always so cheerful."

"I'm not cheerful at all. I'm actually quite troubled."

"You are?" Sabine is delighted. "Do you hate yourself?"

"Sometimes," Nadja says cautiously, regretting the use of "troubled" when she meant to say "somber." She actually said it as half a joke, but Sabine will now hold her to it. "Usually at night, before I fall asleep. Or when I say something I shouldn't have said."

"Like what?"

"Well, like, maybe hurting someone, having said something stupid I didn't really mean. It could be anything, big or small."

"And that's what you mean by troubled?"

"No! That's when I hate myself. You asked if I hate myself."

"Oh, right. So, what do you mean by troubled?"

"Well, I actually meant to say somber. Or worried."

"Then what do you mean exactly by somber?" Sabine will not let go.

"You should have been a lawyer," Nadja says.

"Why?"

"You're cross-examining me."

"I'm not cross-examining you. Talking to you sometimes is like pulling teeth."

They take their breakfast of yogurt and freshly cut fruit out to the porch. The sun is muffled by light fluffy clouds, and now Sabine and Nadja are quiet; they sit and eat in silence. Nadja would like to break the silence, but wants Sabine to break it for a change; Sabine, Nadja knows, is waiting for her to break it.

"Maybe I take you too seriously, too literally," Nadja gives in.

"What do you mean?" Her head bent low over her bowl, Sabine sounds upset, reluctant to speak. Her face is pinched, and Nadja thinks Sabine is about to cry.

"Do you hate me?" Nadja asks, trying, and failing, to lace her voice with a smile.

"I don't hate you," Sabine says.

"But you're upset."

"Of course I'm upset." Sabine finally looks up. "I've asked you a question, and you won't answer. And, what do you mean you take me too literally?"

"When you're negative, or when you say you're depressed. It occurs to me that for you it's just an opening to start a conversation."

"This is pure nonsense. I mean what I say."

"I'm not saying that you don't mean it. I'm just saying that I understand it too literally."

"Let me remind you," Sabine, suddenly inflamed, screams,

"that this entire exchange began when you said you were troubled, and when I tried to figure out what you meant, you balked."

Inside, Nadja feels herself retreat. She avoids looking at Sabine because Sabine turns ugly when she is acting out. Stubbornly, Nadja is staring straight ahead, at the calm and flat water. She is agitated and tries to calm herself. She has never been in therapy and therefore feels she lacks the tools or the ease to discuss these things.

"Listen, Sabine," Nadja says in a controlled, low voice. "Unlike you, I don't always have clear answers. But maybe this confusion, or whatever it is, has to do with my mother. She was easily hurt, I think she felt bullied by her friends, but never voiced a complaint. I know she resented not speaking up, I saw it in her face, and I was angry at her for keeping quiet, for not retaliating. Of course, I never said anything because she was the same with me, always somehow apologetic."

"Maybe," Sabine, mollified, softens her tone, "it had to do with her history? This is how she and generations of Jews survived pogroms and expulsions and camps. It does something to your psyche, having to put up with abuse and keeping your mouth shut."

"Yes," Nadja says. "And it's in our genes, too. That's why I feel guilty when I think about her. I feel guilty but I'm also angry at myself and at her all over again. I also know I should have been more understanding, more of a daughter to her, instead of a cold observer." Nadja sips the last of her coffee and lights a cigarette. "Do you mind?" she asks.

"It's all right." Sabine gives a little shrug. She fiddles with a piece of cantaloupe on her plate. "I don't bully you, do I?"

"Sometimes you do, in your own special way."

Now they turn and look at one another.

"All I wanted to know is what you meant when you said you were troubled," a chastened Sabine explains.

"I'm not sure what I meant," Nadja also strikes a conciliatory note. "It was half a joke, and maybe half a truth. I said it because you accused me of being cheerful all the time, which I know to be untrue."

"But you are. Even if it's forced."

"Well, my dear, one of us has to be, we can't be both glum at the same time, complaining about plumbers and other miscreants."

"I see," Sabine says, and Nadja expects her to smile, but Sabine does not seem to be in the mood.

"What I was trying to say," Nadja continues, "is that I have my down moments, and, you're right, I don't show it, I don't impose it on others. I'm usually alone when I have such moments, when I feel I'm totally alone, detached from people and from life, moments when I feel I'm a failure and that I have no future."

"And then what?"

"And then I fall asleep, and then morning comes and I sit down at my desk and a new day begins."

"Lovely," Sabine grumbles, and Nadja bursts out laughing. "I only wish you'd said it earlier, without me having to pull it out of you."

Nadja nods. "You're right, I'm sorry. Now, enough with the long face. I'll clear the dishes, you get dressed, and we'll go into town. You wanted to get the paper. And I'll buy you ice cream."

Sabine gives her a look. "Are you trying to be nice?"

"With all my heart."

Sabine activates the muscles of her cheeks to show that she

may be willing to smile. "Will you read something I'm working on? I want you to know, I'm insanely jealous when I think of you working nonstop on your novel."

"What are you working on?"

"I don't know yet, but it's the beginning of something. For now it's just words, not even words I think I want to write, but who am I to know for sure. Will you read it?"

"Of course."

"And will you play Scrabble with me later, and be nice to me throughout the day?" Sabine is restored to her demanding self.

"Yes, and yes."

The familiar silence a presence all around her, her things laundered and dried and back in the drawers and closet, Nadja is relieved to be home, alone. She likes the word. She likes the feeling and sound of alone, even if a hint of gloom is also present, a hint she briefly acknowledges, thinking of Marianne Moore's "The cure for loneliness is solitude." Still, some part of her wishes she were back at the cottage with Sabine whose constant chatter always defers other pressing matters. Over ice cream they revisited and settled the issue of cheerful-troubled, with Sabine concluding yet again that Nadja is secretive, and Nadja saying, No, not secretive, but maybe there's a hardness inside her, a hardness she is unwilling, or unable, to break. A hardness that keeps in check bubbles of rage that do sometimes rise to the surface and burst in explosive flames.

She looks out the window: it is a gray and rainy Monday

morning, depressing if you have to schlep to the subway, but perfect to remain quiet and indoors. In her heart she thanks Jerry. Indeed, like he said, she is out of the corporate loop. Now her time is all her own; time, in fact, has acquired a new character. In essence, it is still a source of anxiety, in the sense of Time Passing, but it is no longer bound in large chunks of servility. She wonders if people in the office still mention her in conversations. Probably not. She is gone, forgotten, not even a ghost. Betty may be the only exception, and indeed, Betty is the only one Nadja thinks of once in a while.

She makes coffee and goes to the computer. A slight apprehension, her collaborator, follows behind: now that she has no other commitments, the feeling that she must justify her existence is heightened. She puts her heart and soul into Woman, and yet, again and again, Woman does and says things that are foreign to Nadja, or maybe not so foreign. Woman is merely a character in a book, but she is also quite real. She is serving a purpose, and yet, in the end, it will seem that her life has become so very small, so very insignificant, it will have to be snuffed out. Like a dot on the horizon, Woman will fade and vanish as if she never existed. The police may conduct a short investigation, then drop the case, as just another female found dead in Central Park. No one will miss her and, a week after she is buried, no one will speak her name.

The telephone rings. "It's so good to be back," Raoul says. "I hate being away."

"You missed your office?"

"I missed you. I hate going away and not be able to see you, even if it's only for a week. How was your visit with Sabine?"

"It was good. How was your vacation?" she asks, trying to sound neutral.

"The usual. I'll see you later?"

"I'm here," she says. This morning his words, whether she believes them or not, do not move her, and this is a disconcerting realization. At the beginning, just to hear him say, "I miss you," she thought she could hear and feel his love through the telephone line.

They hang up, and she remains standing by the window. She does not believe Raoul, she does not believe herself. She feels sorry for Raoul, she feels sorry for herself. Back at the computer, she stares at the screen, wondering when leisure and fun have lost their meaning, and obsession took over. But it's a good obsession, Nadja thinks. In his diary Stendhal says: "Let us give ourselves talents," and that's what she is doing, has been doing. She has given herself the talent to persist, to write, to read, to live the way she lives.

And, on the screen, Woman is experiencing a moment of euphoria. She gulps down a couple of vodkas to be ready for him, the man of her dreams; soon, in about an hour, she will see him, may even hold his hand. A charmed marionette, she pirouettes across the screen where she dwells. Silly, silly woman; Nadja feels sorry for her, too.

We're all beggars with dreams, Nadja reflects. Tonight, she and Raoul will have dinner in some expensive restaurant where she will pretend for a short spell that she is living the good life, the same life that all the other, seemingly carefree, diners enjoy. What spoils the illusion for her is the knowledge that she and Raoul are fakes: they are not a couple, and Raoul charges the meals to his expense account. But, she reconsiders, in one way or another, all the diners around them are fakes as well, and so they are all a bunch of fakes faking it in public for each other's benefit.

By now, she and Raoul have a set routine, which may be why stagnation has set in as well, at least in her heart, affecting her spirit and state of mind. Raoul claims that his love for her has grown, and is still growing, but Nadja feels that her love for him has no room to grow and is, in fact, shrinking. So she blames the routine they have fallen into, a routine, she knows, they cannot really change: he arrives, they have a drink, smoke a joint, go out to eat, come back, have sex. When they are in the mood, they will put on some music and dance. Tonight, in all probability, they will skip sex. After they eat, she may want to just drink and wallow, maybe listen to music.

But later, when he arrives in the evening, tan and jaunty in a fall suit, carrying a wet, dripping umbrella, they hug, then sit on the couch and kiss for a long time, and once again she feels the old love, the old arousal, and is grateful for it.

Morning, noon, and night. She lives like a hermit and relishes it. She has always lived frugally, but now she is frugal to the bone, literally aware of every single dollar that leaves her pocket. She walks everywhere, hardly ever takes the bus or train, and draws great satisfaction from the fact that she may walk around town with a ten-dollar bill in her pocket and suddenly realize, a few days later, that the same bill is still there. With a difference, she is now part of a new movement she has learned about on PBS, a group of men and women who have given up their affluent lifestyles and now live simply, growing their own food. Still, sometimes she panics, fearing that her money will run out sooner than expected, and again she reaches for a pen and goes over the numbers to reassure herself, black on white, that she can survive this way for quite some time.

It is two o'clock, and she is out on the street—it is her lunch break—taking in the sights, the sounds. A young girl, sporting a generous cleavage, comes toward her, and Nadja sees herself in the girl, some twenty years ago, walking down the street, half displaying her body, half hiding behind it: half tacky, half shy, maybe half aware. The girl's delicate breast flesh, hoisted and exposed, quivers with every step, and Nadja tries to remember what made her bare her breasts when she was the girl's age. Was it pure delight in her blooming flesh? She remembers one particular summer day, walking down the street in her new bluish-grayish mini dress, acutely and tensely aware of men looking at her a certain way; she felt seductive, self-conscious, and foolish.

She goes back upstairs. Now that she is home all the time, she has begun to pay more attention to her neighbors, is more attentive to doors opening and closing in the hallway. Sometimes, when she thinks she hears an unusual sound, she peers through the peephole, but usually it is just a neighbor taking out the trash.

Vivian is at her door, laughing and talking. All morning, Nadja has been hearing them, possibly out-of-town guests, coming in and out of Vivian's apartment. Now she hears them laugh, she hears the dog howl with contentment.

Mildly jealous, Nadja is thinking: They are having a full day, coming and going. It is Saturday, three o'clock in the afternoon. It is a nice warm day, the sun is shining, and a whole weekend, full of activities, is still ahead of them. While she sits at her desk, where a day begins, and then ends.

And now the couple at the end of the hall is at it again—not a day goes by without the woman screaming at him, and not a peep out of him. Do they ever sleep, Nadja wonders; sometimes she hears them yelling in the early morning. Lately, it seems, things have gotten worse and, a few days ago, one of the neighbors called the police. One day, Nadja is thinking, he will kill the woman, if only to shut her up. They look nearly identical in their long dark hair and narrow dark glasses. They are quite attractive together, and the guy's lean physique and hard-edged cheekbones suggest something of the wolf. He is a musician, and she often hears him go at his guitar behind his door—a discord of mournful sounds. He always seems withdrawn, maybe drugged, and hardly returns her greeting, but this past Fourth of July she met him in the hallway and something compelled her to ask, "Are you going to watch the fireworks tonight?" And he said, "I have enough fireworks in my life," which made her laugh and instantly like him. Some time ago, on her way to the trash chute, she heard them have sex and, unable to stop herself, she approached their door to listen. From the way the woman yowled, Nadja surmised they were doing it doggy-style. She was hoping to hear the guy, but he was as silent as a monk, pushing into the woman, maybe with hate, maybe with love.

That night, back in her apartment, she watched on TV as the giant male tortoise pushed himself onto the female, each thrust accompanied by a long, hard grunt. Tortoises, she learned with wonder and envy, become sexually active only at age fifty, but have a hundred years more to practice.

On the floor above, a young guy died of an overdose. He rotted in his apartment for days until the stench brought in the authorities, the clean-up crews. The guy's dog survived, and a rumor circulated in the building that the hungry dog gnawed on his master's corpse. Now a new tenant has moved in—a fortuitous opportunity for the landlord to raise the rent by thirty percent.

There are no children in their building, only impaired adults living with their pets. And the pets die, too, of disease and heartbreak. A few days ago, getting her mail, she saw her neighbor Ralph, a retired janitor. "Where is your dog?" she asked cheerfully; she usually sees him with a scrawny, grayish poodle.

Ralph looked at her from behind his tinted glasses. "After my wife died, he died." Ralph sniffled, quivering at the mouth. "I found him in the morning, stiff as a log. If you think animals don't miss someone, forget it."

She nodded, painfully embarrassed. She did not even know that he was married, she never saw the wife. And so, the wife passed away. And now the dog. And then Ralph will die, and so on. And the building will live on, its decaying walls recycling humans like so much waste.

What a relentless machine Time is, Nadja thought. She felt awful for Ralph, so thin and frail, now left alone without his wife, without his dog.

"I'm so sorry," she said, and Ralph shook his head and limped away.

The other day, coming home from her lunch break, she was unlocking her door when Vivian's door opened, and Vivian appeared, holding her dog on a short leash. They said, "Hi," then stood there, waiting. Vivian looked stunning, and Nadja wondered where Vivian was headed, and how come she was home this time of the afternoon. She was wearing high heels, black tights, and a beautiful leather jacket. Her wavy dark hair was loose on her shoulders, and large sunglasses, covering half her face, sat on her nose.

"Playing hooky?" Vivian finally asked.

"Huh, not exactly," Nadja replied. "I was fired a few weeks ago."

"Really? Wow." Vivian tossed her hair away from her face, while pulling the leash on the dog. "Sit down, Ben," she told the dog. Some women, Nadja mused, have this look—hard, and fiercely independent. Their look says: Don't mess with me! Nadja often wishes she had that kind of look. "Any prospects for another job?"

Nadja glanced at the dog, a large and energetic German shepherd with sad brown eyes. "Not yet. I'm taking it easy for a while. His name is Ben?"

"Yeah." Vivian yanked on the leash. "Sit," she commanded, and this time the dog obeyed. "He's so mulish." Vivian laughed. "Unless you tell him six times, he doesn't believe you really mean it. So, you're taking time off. That's great. I wish I could take time off. I'm playing hooky today."

"Good for you." She has a good face, Nadja observed further. Strong, sensuous nostrils, a wide mouth. "You know what Thoreau said."

"Thoreau?"

"The writer?"

"Oh, yeah," Vivian said vaguely, and Nadja felt stupid. "What did he say?"

"He said that no matter how much we get paid, employees, as a rule, get screwed."

"How true. Why don't you come in sometime? For coffee? Or something stronger?"

"Something stronger."

Vivian smiled, nodding, assessing. "Great. Just tell me when is good."

So, yes, Nadja reflects. She is turning into a new person—friendlier, less harried, even gregarious. She actually looks forward to talking with her neighbors, to establishing new contacts. She has also developed a new relationship with her mailbox, the postman, and the superintendent of the building. A few times a day, it suddenly dawns on her that she is not in an office and that she need not hide in the bathroom, or answer to a Jerry. This is the first time in her adult life that she does not have to get up in the morning and report to work, and it is amazing to her that she, the minion, has actually pulled it off. At least for the time being.

Aside from the dinners they share, now Raoul, as a matter of routine, brings his leftover lunch, usually steaks, or whatever she tells him in advance, sometimes Italian, sometimes Chinese. She is still at the computer when he arrives, so she tells him, "Put it in the freezer," and he says, "Oh, you and your freezer," and she laughs.

She is in good spirits. She is having a good workday. She looks forward to seeing Raoul in the evening, but Raoul calls and, from the sound of his voice, she knows he is calling to cancel.

"Hi, darling."

"Hi."

"How are you sweetheart?"

"I'm okay." She is sprawled in the armchair, feeling mellow, having swallowed a couple of Advils to ease her cramps. "I just got my period, so no sex tonight."

"No, no sex tonight," he repeats. "Lydia wants me home."

"What happened?"

"Nothing special, I don't think, she's just feeling a bit down, probably something that happened at work. I told you, she doesn't like her job."

"Why doesn't she quit? You make enough money."

"Not in her mind. She thinks we're poor."

"Amazing. I think she likes her job more than she knows."

"Maybe." Raoul is quiet. Possibly comparing the two women in his life. Possibly wishing for peace and quiet. "Will I see you tomorrow?"

He sounds tired, maybe indeed tired of women. It occurs to Nadja that Raoul is making up a story, just as he does when he calls Lydia to tell her he will be late. "Are you sure you'll be going straight home tonight?"

"Where else would I be going?"

"I don't know, a new mistress?"

Pleased, Raoul laughs. "You think too highly of me."

"I do."

"Tomorrow?"

"Tomorrow."

They hang up, and Nadja realizes that she is actually glad to have the evening all to herself. She will have a quiet dinner, will watch her quiet TV. Maybe this is how Lydia feels when Raoul calls with an excuse. It is a chilly, sunless day, and she lingers a while longer before she rises from the armchair and goes back to her desk. Her real life, she reflects, happens precisely when she is not engaged in life or thinking about life.

In Stuyvesant Town Park, leaves turn yellow and fall to the ground. It is eight o'clock in the morning, and Nadja is taking her morning walk-trot. The three old ladies she has come to cherish as her old ladies are there, too, walking briskly, and the tall one among them, as usual, does all the talking. One day, Nadja knows, she, too, will be old, will look old, but she is also thankful that this eventuality does not truly sink in, not yet, it is just a passing thought. And these three old ladies are different from her and her friends. These women, it is obvious, have raised families; it was their first priority. Nadja and her friends are single and childless. They have learned early on to preserve and cultivate a youthful look—their first priority?

Grave-looking men and women, carrying briefcases, tote-bags, backpacks, go past her, on their way to work. Nadja looks at them, trying to recapture her sense of misery when she was in their shoes. She is struck by the thought that while they have to rush to work, she, the bum, can loiter in the park. She can stand all morning, if she so chooses, and watch several grackles take a shower under a dripping faucet. Watching the birds, it is clear that they know the meaning of standing in line and waiting your turn. In the past weeks, she has had a couple of dreams where she is back in the office, and seemingly quite happy. They had called and asked her to come back and she did, she went back, working part-time. In the dream, it suddenly hits her that she does not want to be there—why did she agree to go back? How is she going to extricate herself? At this point, she wakes up, as if from a nightmare.

She sits for a while on a bench, feasting her eyes on the remaining leaves on the trees and listening to the quiet in her head. She then rises and walks around the oval, rotating her arms. An old lady, coming toward her, laughs and says, "You're terrific," and Nadja, seeing in this woman a divine messenger, happily says, "Thank you!"

Later, at her desk, Nadja watches Woman who is talking to herself in the mirror. The mirror talks back, mirroring, and Nadja, jittery and anxious, is also spinning in mirrors; something, she does not know what, gnaws at her. Maybe Woman annoys her. Rehearsing, Woman raises her hand and kisses it, pretending to be kissing the man, all the while observing herself in the mirror and trying to see what she looks like when her head is inclined just so as she is passionately kissing the man she has chosen to love. As Nadja stares at Woman, the telephone rings out. Sabine's voice sounds in the room. Nadja hesitates, then picks up the call.

"What's up?"

"Nothing," Sabine mutters. "I love the way you greet your friends. It's insulting, you know."

Nadja takes a long, meditative breath, telling herself to be patient, nothing is burning. "I'm working, Sabine. All I said was, What's up. It's colloquial. Like, what's up?"

"I told you, nothing, I just want to talk. To a friend." Sabine's voice is subdued. "Believe it or not, I worry about you, that's all. You drive yourself too hard. You're too isolated. I think you're headed for a mental breakdown."

Nadja is filled with sudden joy. "No, dear. But why do you say such a thing?"

"Oh, just meanness, cruelty."

"No, I think you truly care about me, but it's so deep down..."

Sabine makes a chortling sound. "No, sweetie, it's just selfishness and self-loathing. Do you think you're a great writer? Do you care about posterity?"

"Don't you?"

"I used to, but I'm losing it to commerce. You have to be cynical in this age."

"I think I'm cynical when I need to be."

"No, sweetie, you're not. You're naïve, you believe in people."

"Is it bad?"

"Beyond redemption."

Nadja thinks of Woman, waiting in limbo on the screen.

Sabine, after a pause. "You won't talk to me."

"I am talking to you."

"But you're dying to get back to your little novel."

Nadja decides to ignore "little." "Well, yes, I left her hanging."

"How's she doing?"

"She is getting herself all worked up."

"About?"

"Oh, silly man stuff. She thinks she is in love."

"You know," Sabine says, "you should pay more attention to your friends. Your friends love you."

Nadja laughs. "What's the matter with you?"

"I don't know. My usual non-state. Maybe I'll take a nap. You should live more, by the way."

"I'm living."

Nadja is ready to hang up, but Sabine, in her shrewdness, offers bait. "I did call to tell you something..."

"Well??"

"I finally got laid, if you can believe it."

"A small miracle! Mazel tov!"

"It wasn't great or anything, it's someone I met through the Internet. We weren't compatible, she had the wrong energy, but I let her do things to me."

"What things?"

"I let her give me a blowjob."

Nadja is tantalized, but keeps her voice even. "What did you do for her?"

"I opened my legs." Sabine pauses, as if waiting for Nadja to get it, but Nadja does not. "It's a gift, dear."

Nadja, surprised, giggles with delight. "Do you negotiate these things beforehand?"

"What do you mean?"

"Like who will do what for whom? Or, what you will or won't do?"

"Sort of."

Nadja hears soft tapping sounds on the other end. "Are you typing as we speak?"

"I'm just dealing with my e-mail. I feel so demoralized. Just think of the last two weeks. First, the not-so-hot Internet person, second, the woman who stood me up last week, third, the date I changed my sheets for and the bitch wouldn't even come home with me. Nobody wants me, I feel so old."

"At least you're putting yourself out there, you meet people. And, you're only forty-something. If you think about it, life expectancy is being revised almost daily and with all these new drugs on the market we may live to be a hundred and fifty. In that case, you're still an infant."

"That's not the issue. The dyke scene is very hot these days, much more than it was when I was growing up. Today it's hip to hit the clubs, you meet cool people, but they're all so young, they won't even look at me. In my time, it was mostly a bridge and tunnel crowd."

"You're a baby-boomer. There are many baby-boomers out there, aging with you."

"I suppose." A deep sigh. "I hate my chichi friends, I'm sick and tired of the scene. I'm bored with writing, I'm bored with everything. Nobody loves me."

"I love you."

"I know, sweetie."

"I wish I could do more, but you're so far away. Take a valium."

"I already did."

"How's the weather? Can you go for a swim?"

"I don't feel like taking a swim. I think I'll take a nap. Call me sometime."

"I will, little one, I promise."

After they hang up, Nadja, deciding to take a break from *Woman*, picks up Jane Bowles's *Two Serious Ladies*, a novel she is rereading for the third time. Miss Goering is in bad shape. She is having drinks with the big man who keeps insisting, in spite of her protestations, that she is a working prostitute. Not a small-time prostitute, but a medium one. Miss Goering laughs: she had no idea she looked like a prostitute, she says. A derelict perhaps, or an escaped lunatic, but not a prostitute. The man's chauffeur drives them to the man's house, where they are served steaks. From there, they drive to a restaurant where the man has a meeting with three brutal-looking men; Miss Goering is to sit at a table by herself and wait. Bored, she calls Mrs. Copperfield, who, indeed, is back from Panama and is delighted to hear from her friend. Mrs. Copperfield arrives with Pacifica, who reminds Miss Goering of her own Miss Gamelon, although Pacifica, Miss Goering has to admit, is a much nicer person and physically more attractive. Mrs. Copperfield, Miss Goering notes, is terribly thin and seems to suffer from a skin eruption. She is as high strung as ever, gulping down her double whiskeys, occasionally spilling some on her chin; Mrs. Copperfield confides that she has gone to pieces, something she has wanted to do for years.

Something she has wanted to do for years, Nadja thinks. Allow herself to go to pieces. An anarchic aggression directed at the self. Nadja at times experiences such an impulse, she is aware of it when she gives in to it, when she suddenly needs to rebel against herself, against her mostly neat and orderly and rational life. She lets go, but not for long, and she does not venture too far. She always comes back, has never allowed herself to go all the way to the other side.

All at once, she feels tears coming on, and she rises and goes to the bathroom to stem the flow. What is it with her? And why the sudden tears, out of nowhere? Maybe Sabine is right, she's working too much. She'll take a puff on a joint and go out for a walk. Then, if she feels like it, she'll go back to work. She's an adult, she has a brain. It's all right to break down once in a while, and, it could be her period, she's more emotional when she has her period. And later, Raoul is coming. He'll cheer her up. But, first thing first: a toke, and then out the door.

I feel antsy."

"I can tell." Raoul, looking miserable, sits in the armchair. Nadja is on the couch.

Looking over at Raoul, she feels cruel. "You bore me. We have nothing to say to each other. If I don't initiate a conversation, we don't talk. Your brain is empty, and you won't even make an effort."

Raoul crosses his legs. "What can I tell you, Nadja? This is the brain I have. Maybe not as good as yours, but the only one I have."

This is true, she thinks, what does she want from him? "It's comical, isn't it? The way we sit here, discussing your brain."

"I don't know, maybe it is. It wasn't my idea."

She smiles, and this cheers her up somewhat. She is feeling hopeful. Maybe she can still change things around and save the evening. "You can smile," she tells him.

"I don't feel like smiling."

Nadja's smile fades. She tries to imagine how she would feel if Raoul were to sit there and tell her that he did not love her, if Raoul were to tell her that she was boring.

She says nothing, now sharing in his misery. If they were a normal couple, they would not feel they had to engage in conversation: he would be doing his thing, she would be doing hers. Just like he is with Lydia, the two of them sitting in separate rooms, watching different programs on TV. She conjures up an image of Raoul, years from now, in a nursing home, an old man in a wheelchair. And where will she be? Possibly already dead, or, miraculously, an active old maid.

Raoul speaks in a low voice. "Maybe we need a break from one another. Maybe you should try to meet other people. I don't want to stand in your way."

He may be right. They have discussed this a few times in the past. One day, they both know, they will have to part. They will be friends, they promise one another, and maybe they will be.

Looking at him, Nadja realizes that she has not touched his face in a very long time. Sitting cross-legged, she becomes aware of a faint odor she recognizes as the odor of her menstrual blood. She wonders if Raoul recognizes the odor and what it means to him. She recalls a middle-aged woman, a neighbor who moved out a couple of years ago. The woman had a terrible odor, a strong vaginal odor, and Nadja thought the woman masturbated a lot.

"What are you thinking about?" Raoul breaks the silence.

"My period."

"What about it?"

"Can you smell it?"

"Not from here."

"Want to come closer?"

"You know I do."

He comes and joins her on the couch; they cuddle.

"Why are you so mean?"

"I don't know. I'm stuck."

"Stuck how?"

"My novel. I'm not sure about the ending."

"Are you there already?" Raoul is surprised.

"No. But I feel I should have some idea where she is going. Decisions have to be made, you know. It's a matter of life and death."

"Well, it's not real death," Raoul says.

"Of course it's real. It's very real to her."

Raoul thinks a moment. "You're right, I wasn't thinking. I think it'll come to you. Your brain is working on it, and it will come."

"I hope so." Nadja smiles. "Not bad for a layperson."

Now Raoul is smiling too. "I've been around you long enough. Is this what they call a writer's block?"

"It's a thinking block."

"Does she have to die? The woman in your novel?"

"No, she doesn't, but I think she is working toward it, almost inviting it. She is too desperate, too eager, too hungry."

"Well, we'll have to wait and see, she may yet fool you. But," Raoul continues, "I can tell it's not just your novel. Something else is going on with you, but you won't tell me."

"I am telling you. It's my novel. It's the only thing I care about."

"Thanks."

"It's not exactly what I meant, and you know it."

"I do. But I wish you were more cheerful."

"That's funny. Sabine complains that I'm too cheerful."

"Well, I can just imagine what her idea of cheerful is. If you're not sobbing and tearing your hair out then you're too cheerful."

Nadja laughs, and Raoul seems to revive. "Do you want to go eat?" he asks.

"I'm not really hungry. Are you?"

"Not right now, no."

"So let's just sit here for a while and talk."

"And kiss?"

"Only if you promise to kiss me the way teenagers kiss."

"It's a deal."

Ben, barking and wagging his tail, is crowding the doorway. "I'm so glad you came," Vivian says, trying to hold on to Ben to make room for Nadja. "Come in, come in."

Nadja walks inside, careful not to stumble over Ben who is obviously very glad to see her. "Dogs are so emotional," she says.

"Expressively so! Imagine if people greeted each other like

dogs do." Vivian shuts the door. "Sometimes I wish I were a dog. It takes so little to make them happy."

In the living room, Nadja sits down on the futon, and Ben, having received a firm command from Vivian, follows his mistress into the kitchen. Nadja leans back and looks over the room. To her relief, everything looks and smells clean, no unpleasant odors to interfere with her nose when Vivian brings in the drinks and munchies.

Vivian's apartment is the same one bedroom as Nadja's, except that one of her walls is exposed brick. There is a large potted plant in the corner near the window, and a couple of framed Georgia O'Keefe posters are hanging on the wall. No books, though, no bookshelves, and Nadja worries that she may have nothing to say to her neighbor. She discovers a small fish tank, next to the TV set, and lets herself be mesmerized by a couple of gold fish darting back and forth; so they do have something in common, even if Nadja's fish died long ago. As she is thinking these thoughts, an enormous calico cat comes out of the bedroom, and Nadja, acting friendly, extends her hand for a sniff, a gesture the cat finds too forward and instantly retreats; she gives Nadja one more serious look and leaves the room.

"Sorry I'm taking so long." Vivian appears in the kitchen door. "I hope you're not bored?"

"Oh, no, I'm fine, I'm looking at your fish. I used to have a fish once. I still have the tank."

"Really? Just one fish?" Vivian disappears in the kitchen, then reappears, carrying a large tray.

"Yes, just one." Nadja watches as Vivian puts down the tray on the coffee table. "Everything looks so yummy," Nadja adds.

"Thanks." Vivian begins to uncork a bottle of wine, a Merlot. "I hope you like kielbasa." She points at the tray.

"I love kielbasa. And the bread, too, is my kind of bread."

"Sunflower bread. I get it at the Farmers Market."

Nadja wets her lips. Everything looks much better than she hoped. The kielbasa, the bread, the sliced red and yellow peppers, the cherry tomatoes on the stem. "What kind of cheese is it?"

"Saint Simone." Vivian laughs. "Looks like a breast, doesn't it?"

"Yes it does!"

Vivian uncorks the bottle in a swift, clean motion; there is a sense of a clean finish to everything she does. Vivian pours the wine; they click glasses and smile.

"It's very good," Nadja says, now feeling a bit contrite. She is the worst guest. She shouldn't have come empty-handed. She never does, but Vivian insisted she must bring nothing but herself.

"Thank you. Go ahead and eat, don't wait for me." Vivian lights a cigarette, then blows the smoke to the ceiling. "I'll join you in a minute."

Tempted by the airy nonchalance of leaning back and smoking, Nadja considers delaying eating and asking for a cigarette, but she is hungry. Trying to not appear too eager, she cuts a slice of kielbasa, then watches as Vivian, with a contented sigh, slumps in the low chair across from Nadja and stretches out her legs. "God, I'm beat, what a crazy day."

Vivian is wearing a white T-shirt and black sweat pants. Her hair is pulled back in a ponytail, and her face is clean of makeup; Nadja feels a sudden urge to tell her neighbor that she is even more attractive without makeup.

"What do you do?" Nadja asks.

"I'm a nurse," Vivian says.

A nurse. This is a surprise. In a medical emergency, she could knock on Vivian's door.

"And you? Before you were fired?" Vivian asks.

"I don't really have a profession," Nadja says. "I worked for this accounting firm, and they trained me as a librarian. I have a graduate degree in English."

"Ah," Vivian says. "English."

"Indeed." Nadja laughs. "Not very practical or profitable in our world, but no other subject interested me. How does one become a nurse?"

"I don't know." Vivian shrugs. "I fell into it somehow. A good friend of mine went to nursing school, so I went, too, just for something to do. I didn't give it much thought, I just did it, not really planning long-term ahead, like, you know, being a nurse forever, but here I am, ten years later. It's hard work, but I'm good at it. And the money is good." She leans forward and stubs out her cigarette. "How's the kielbasa?

"Delicious. Everything is just right."

"Super." Vivian cuts two hefty slices of kielbasa and makes a sandwich for herself. The cat comes over, and Vivian, gently, nudges her away with her elbow.

"What's her name?" Nadja asks.

"Jerry." Chewing and smiling, Vivian looks at Nadja. "Like the ice cream?"

"The ice cream?" Nadja says, and then she gets it. "Of course! I didn't immediately connect the Ben with the Jerry. I'm kind of slow sometimes, and I got stuck on the Jerry. My boss's name was Jerry."

"Oh."

"A real ass, yes," Nadja says, hoping for an appreciative response from Vivian, but Vivian, a vigorous eater once she gets started, is focused on her sandwich.

Nadja reaches for a piece of cheese and bread. "You run a nice little zoo," she ventures.

"A zoo?"

"A dog, a cat, fish. It must be time-consuming, feeding them every morning, and shopping for and schlepping all those cans."

Vivian scrutinizes her, sort of amused. "All those cans?"

"In the supermarket. You see them all the time at the checkout counter. That's how you recognize them, you know, pet owners. Same as parents, loading their carts with Formula and diapers. It must cost a small fortune, raising babies, pets."

Vivian laughs, and Nadja is relieved.

"You're funny, Nadja," Vivian says.

"Funny ha-ha, or funny strange?"

"Both."

Now Nadja laughs, pleased. She pours more wine into her glass; Vivian's is still half full. "My good friend Sabine says I'm too detached from life."

"So? What exactly does it mean?"

"I'm not sure. I think she's trying to tell me I don't live enough."

"What do you think?"

"I think I live okay. Maybe not enough, but quite alright. I don't see many people. Most of the time I prefer to stay home."

"Me, too, actually. By the way, this guy who visits you once in a while, he's your boyfriend, no?"

"Yes."

"He seems nice. Is he married?"

Nadja, surprised, feels herself blush. "How did you know?"

Vivian shrugs her shoulders and gives Nadja a naughty little smile. "Well, it's quite obvious. He's never around on weekends, and he wears suits."

"Oh. What's wrong with suits?"

"Nothing. But he has this look, the business look, and those types are usually married. And, they don't live in this neighborhood."

"True. What about you? Are you seeing someone?"

"At the moment, no one special." Vivian lights another cigarette, and Nadja observes the wide mouth, the high cheekbones, the muddy green eyes. Vivian's features, she reflects, are savage, untamed. She tries to visualize Vivian in a dour nurse uniform.

Vivian exhales. "So what do you do all day, now that you're out of work?"

"I'm trying to write a book."

"Cool."

"We'll see." Nadja points at the walls. "Where do you hide your books?"

"I read and give them away. Mostly detectives and science fiction. What kind of book are you writing?"

"It's a novel. I think it might be read as a psychological thriller, even though I don't think of it as a thriller."

"I'd love to read it when you're done." Vivian takes a mouthful of wine. "Are you okay for money? I hope your boyfriend helps you with the rent. It's only fair, right? At least in my book it is."

Nadja smiles, appreciating Vivian's directness. "Yes, he does, and I have some savings and I'm also getting unemployment. I often fantasize that thanks to some computer glitch, these checks will keep coming, maybe forever. Or maybe I'll sell my book, which is like saying I'll win the lottery."

"You've got to believe in yourself," Vivian says earnestly.

"Well, yes, I do, and then I don't, depending."

"Like the rest of us. Would you like some coke?"

"Coke?"

"Cocaine," Vivian enunciates.

"Medicine." Nadja smiles.

"Yup."

"I prefer pot."

"I have pot."

Vivian brings out a small leather pouch from a basket under the table and is soon rolling a joint; Nadja is intent on Vivian's large competent hands, her somewhat coarse knuckles. "I think I'm a little high already."

"Wow." Vivian looks up. "You haven't even drunk that much."

"I had a sip of vodka at home. When I'm nervous, I get drunk faster."

"Are you nervous?"

"I was. About coming here. I didn't know… you know…"

"I know, I was nervous, too." Vivian laughs. "We're so finicky and cautious about everything, about other people, as if we were so different, or so much better than they." Vivian hands Nadja a fat joint. "Here, I already had some before, it's all yours."

"Thanks. I only need a puff or two," Nadja says, and soon she is coughing, handing the joint back to Vivian, who puts it away and prepares a line for herself.

"On second thought." Nadja chuckles, a bit self-conscious. "Maybe I could try some." She points at the coke.

"Be my guest."

Nadja bends over the powder and inhales, feeling a tickle in her throat and nostrils. She has tried cocaine a couple of times before, and it did nothing for her, but now, all at once, her heart is pounding. She ate too fast, she thinks. And maybe drank too much and too fast. And the pot. True debauchery. Now all she wants to do is to lie down and shut her eyes. Indeed, she is the worst guest. A strange, bird-like clarity spreads in her brain, and a sudden paranoia sets in about Vivian, about her possible ulterior motives.

What ulterior motives? Vivian is a neighbor, a nurse, hospitable, offering her free food and drugs. Whatever happens, she is only a few steps away from her own living room. Her phone may be ringing, and her loyal machine collects the messages and saves them for her.

"Are you all right?" Vivian asks.

"Yes. Do you mind if I lie down?"

"Not at all."

Nadja stretches out on the futon and leans on her elbow. Vivian bends over a line, then raises her head to the ceiling. She smiles at Nadja. "Want some more?"

"No, I think I'm totally fine."

"Are you tired?"

"No. Maybe a little."

"In case you're wondering, I don't do this very often, only on special occasions."

"It must be quite expensive."

"Well, yes," Vivian says, "life is expensive."

"You know." Nadja sits up. "I pick up pennies and dimes, sometimes even quarters." Vivian is looking at her quizzically. "On the street. When I see a penny, I pick it up. I keep them in circulation."

"That's very good of you."

Nadja laughs. "Street people congratulate me when they see

me do it. They say, God bless you! I used to pick up pennies only when they were heads up, but now tails is fine, too. I figure I can collect about twenty bucks a year."

"Hallelujah." Vivian undoes her ponytail and shakes out her hair. "Let me put some music on."

Vivian puts on Chemical Brothers, and Nadja stretches out on the futon and shuts her eyes. Shapes are moving behind her lids, looping with the music. She has the sense that nearby, on the carpet, Vivian is lying down, too. Nadja wonders if she should be on guard, if there is something sexual about the two of them lying down like this, with abandon. She revisits an image of Raoul standing in his boxer shorts in the middle of her living room, sucking on a fat cigar and fondling his balls. Raoul, now again on Cape Cod for a few days, playing husband, father; Nadja wonders if he remembers to be sad and bored without her. She wonders if his odor changes, if he becomes a totally different man. He says she is the only person in the world who truly knows him, and it may be true. He may be saying this to please her, or to please himself. Lydia and the kids probably know another real Raoul, just as real as the one she believes she knows.

"Remember Doug?" Nadja hears Vivian whisper.

"No."

"The guy who died? On the floor above?"

"Oh, yes."

"I spent the night with him once. I freaked when he died."

"Yes, it was awful. I didn't really know him, but it was awful."

"Sad," Vivian says.

Woman appears in her mind, and Nadja sees her bound in a net on the kitchen floor of a wealthy art collector. He has just fed her a sumptuous meal, and now Woman, like a fish, is trapped in a net. This is only one image, but Nadja can start there, or get there, once she has a better idea what Woman is up to, or up against. Woman is attractive, maybe like Vivian, but is vulnerable and easy to hurt. She is a tax lawyer, but just as likely she could have been a nurse, a librarian. She could give Woman Vivian's strong face, or maybe Deirdre's more refined features, Deirdre's oddly sad lips.

Her old friend Deirdre. They have not spoken or seen one another in months. Deirdre sometimes goes into "hibernation," as she calls it—she withdraws from the world, telling friends not to call her. When she is ready, she reemerges, and is social again. Funny that she is thinking about Deirdre. Funny that she is on the verge of allowing herself to fall asleep on Vivian's futon. Maybe the futon is the clue. Deirdre also favors futons. Another funny thought: What if Vivian ties her up, right here, on the futon?

"What are you thinking about?" she hears Vivian ask, and Nadja opens her eyes. She was wrong. Vivian is still sitting in the low chair, smoking a cigarette. Ben and Jerry, like sculpted guards, are perched on either side of her.

"My protagonist." Slowly, Nadja raises herself, resisting an urge to rub her eyes. "She is very foolish, the romantic type. She worries me."

"Why?"

"The guy she is with may turn out to be a weirdo."

"There are many weirdoes out there."

"Yeah."

"Can't she tell he's a weirdo?"

"Not yet. She wants to be in love and lose herself. Or maybe just to lose herself."

"I know women like her," Vivian says. "Actually, years ago,

I went out on a date with a man who practically kidnapped me. He had me in his car and kept driving around, wondering aloud if he should kill me. Believe it or not, when he finally let me go, I felt sorry for him."

"Wow. Did you report him?"

"No. I was young, I didn't know better, and I also thought, after it was over and I was free and safe, that it was kind of an exotic and interesting experience. Not to be repeated, of course."

Now Vivian sprawls herself on the carpet, and Ben and Jerry adjust to Vivian's new position.

"On the whole," Vivian continues, "I feel grateful for the people I met in my life, even those who were not good for me, and others I don't see anymore because we had a fight, or whatever. With most of them, it was good while it lasted. They all left their mark."

"I feel this way, too," Nadja says. "People say we learn from our mistakes, but I don't think we actually do." She lies down again and shuts her eyes. Maybe Woman has a death wish. Maybe everyone has it, a need to test the distance between the poles of life and death.

How good it feels, lying here, on Vivian's futon, aware of the beat of the music and thinking about Woman. There is a lot she can do for Woman, there is a lot Woman can do for her. She looks forward to tomorrow when she'll rise and sit down at her desk.

Nadja sits up. "Do you have to work tomorrow?"

"Unfortunately."

"What time do you start?"

"Early. Seven o'clock."

"Seven o'clock! I'd better leave and let you get some sleep."

"Whenever. No sweat."

"Next time you come to me."

"Sure. Just say the word."

The following morning, watering her plants, Nadja feels a sudden uplift. She will take a day off and sit in the park and read a book. She will take Woman, too, just in case she decides to do some work; both she and Woman may benefit. A pale, hesitant sun stands in the sky, maybe still waking. A few of the early-morning regulars are already there when she arrives: the serene-looking Asian man, in his 60s or 70s. His takeout coffee at his side, he sits on a bench and contemplates the trunk of a tree: absolute stillness. He then reaches into his pocket, lights a cigarette, draws deeply and holds it in and then slowly exhales. A couple of elderly Asian women doing their tai chi routine, one of them is the obvious guide, as the other watches and follows her movements. An older white man, tall and wearing a red bandana, watches the two women from a distance and also tries to follow. A groundskeeper is sweeping leaves off the path. A woman pushing a stroller goes past Nadja's bench. The little girl in the stroller says, "Daddy?" and mother answers, "Daddy is at work, sweetie."

Nadja is all contentment. More and more she feels she is changing, becoming more accepting, more easy-going, more intent on pleasure and less haunted by thoughts of work. She has no desire to read, or look at Woman. She just wants to sit and watch. Work and diligence can wait.

Once a year, during the High Holidays, Nadja gets to feel Jewish with other Jews. Luckily, there is a synagogue a couple of blocks from her home and it is just a quick walk back and forth. She holds a prayer book in her hands and, leafing through the pages, comes across a caption that reads: "People who read the words of prayer with great devotion may come to see the light within the letters, even though they may not understand the meaning of the words they speak."

Nadja reads it again, then raises her head from the book. A musty odor hangs in the crowded synagogue, a sure indication that most of the congregants, unlike Nadja, obey the directive not to bathe and not to brush their teeth. Nadja's belief in God is sporadic, but mourning rituals do hold a meaning for her, and she is in the synagogue for the Yizkor service to commemorate her parents who had mourned their parents and relatives who had perished in the camps. She is also supposed to atone for her sins, and in her own way she does, asking forgiveness for potential and actual offenses she may have committed. Still, she feels somewhat uncomfortable and self-conscious when required to beat her chest with her fist while reciting the long litany of wrongdoings listed in the prayer book. But everyone around her is doing it, so she does it, too.

It is a small synagogue, and Nadja tries to estimate how many people are present. Churches, she reflects, and especially cathedrals, are hushed, spacious and elegant, what with their high ceilings, the heavy chandeliers, the stained-glass windows, the grand oil paintings depicting saints, the strong scent of burning incense. In the church, the feeling is of reserve and decorum, whereas in the synagogue—usually just a room or a hall—there is a prevalent feeling of ordered chaos, with babies crying, people talking and walking in and out, just as in the home of a large family.

The beautiful voice of the cantor rises as she recites the Kaddish. She looks small and slender on the stage, and is draped, like a saint, in a long white robe, which makes Nadja think of the Ku Klux Klan. The cantor has been fasting since yesterday evening, and yet her voice is strong and clear. Nadja used to fast when growing up, it was a challenge among her friends, but now she allows herself coffee and fruit. This morning she showered and brushed her teeth, and had her coffee at the computer. At this very moment, Woman is raving and ranting in the net. The man, Woman believes, is recording the scene of her wretched humiliation with hidden cameras. He must have a collection of such recordings, she thinks with despair; indeed, she is nothing special, she is one of many. A fool with a law degree. She begs him to release her, but she may as well be talking to the walls, which, in actual fact, may be the case, since she cannot see her tormentor. The net is tight against her skin, against her face, and she cannot open her eyes.

After the Yizkor service, Nadja walks home, but she will return in the evening for the Nehila service. Most of the congregation will remain in the synagogue, atoning, praying, and when night falls and the men and boys on the Bima blow their shofars to signal the end of the fast, how exhilarated they will feel for having endured. They will rush home for the festive meal, F & F at the center of their lives: family and food. Nadja, too, looks forward to the evening meal: she will have pasta and salad and a glass of red wine, while watching the news.

The telephone rings. "Are you fasting?" Sabine asks.

"More or less. I drink coffee and eat fruit."

"So, you don't smoke."

"I don't buy them anymore, but I did smoke half a cigarette."

"It doesn't count as fasting if you smoke."

"The new rabbi on the block?"

"It won't kill you not to smoke on Yom Kippur."

"I do it my own way, Sabine, everybody does."

"Who is everybody?"

"People like us, secular year round, but come Yom Kippur we all grab a Torah."

Sabine chuckles. "I do it by the book, like a true Orthodox."

"That's because you're a good Jew and God loves you."

Another chuckle. "Making fun of your friend on Yom Kippur. Let's break fast together, I'm taking you out."

"You're in town?"

"Obviously."

"All right, but I don't want some exotic Asian fare."

"No, sweetie, we'll go Jewish, kosher."

"By the way, dear," the thought occurs to Nadja. "If you do it by the book, you shouldn't be talking on the phone, you know. You should be in synagogue."

There's a long pause, then Sabine says, "I was in synagogue earlier, but, you're right, I forgot about the phone."

Toward evening, the two Yahrzeit candles that have been burning in Nadja's kitchen since the evening before, flicker their last flames. Lightly, Nadja kisses the still hot glass containers, just in case the containers are holy, just in case they held her parents, then places them in the recycling bin.

At Veselka they order chicken soup, schnitzel, mashed potatoes. It is not exactly kosher, but it is close enough. Nadja is not very hungry, and it feels a bit lonely, breaking fast in Veselka. One is supposed to be with one's family, but Nadja is an orphan, and Sabine's parents do not celebrate the holidays, which upsets

Sabine quite a lot. They talk about the title Woman Ending Badly, and why Nadja chose it.

"Well," Nadja says, "I have this idea about women in trouble of their own making. Women who end badly because of their own gullibility and poor judgment. In fiction and in life."

"They do, but I'm not sure anyone would want to read it."

"Well, thanks, that's exactly what I need to hear."

"Sorry, sweetie, I didn't mean it this way. What I meant, and I think Virginia Woolf said it, is that when women begin to write the truth about their lives, the world will split open. Or something like that."

"It was actually Muriel Rukeyser," Nadja says.

"Whoever. My point was that people will find it hard to read."

"Well." Nadja is reminded of Jane Bowles. "I've been rereading *Two Serious Ladies*."

Sabine makes a face. "You like her?"

"I love her."

"Something must be the matter with me, but I like Paul Bowles better."

"Something is the matter with you. She was a far better writer. The same is true of Veza Canetti—again, a much better writer than her husband. But the wives died young and the men lived to be old and famous men."

"You know," Sabine says. "I've been thinking about you, about our conversations, like when we talked about your mother being passive, and that you hated it, and our conversations about your father, and it suddenly hit me that you have an unusual mix of secrecy, no, reticence, reticence and openness."

Nadja looks at Sabine. "This is probably the nicest thing you ever said to me," she says, and Sabine's face takes on the most amazing expression—she seems taken aback and gratified at the same time. She may even be blushing under her tan. In fact, Nadja is blushing too.

"Are you sure?" Sabine asks.

"Positive. And possibly the wisest thing, too."

At this, Sabine's eyes twinkle with mischief. "I seriously doubt it," she says, and the two of them start laughing as one, happy for having got over the hump of too-close-for-comfort intimacy, relieved they can now go back to the present moment, back to their usual selves again.

"By the way," Nadja says. "What I didn't tell you about my mother is that I do have good memories of her. Especially two that sometimes just appear in my mind, as if to make sure I don't forget them. Now that I think of it, it makes sense to me that both take place at the kitchen table, and in both I'm about six or seven and I feel this deep love for her, the love of a six-year-old. Very strange."

"What's strange?"

"That I remember it so clearly. Not only the time and place but the deep love I felt for her. Do you want to hear them?"

"Of course! After such an introduction how could I not. Besides, I love hearing about your parents."

"All right," Nadja says, feeling her face soften as she conjures her mother's face. "In one, she is wrapping each cover of my school books with glossy paper. I'm leaning against the table and watch her face, her hands, and think how good she is to do this for me, and that I could never do it as beautifully as she."

"Why was she wrapping the covers?"

"To protect the books. They were school property and we had to return them at the end of the year."

Sabine nods. "And the second?"

"I think in this one I must have stayed home from school, down with a cold or something, because no one was home, just the two of us, and we sit at the table and she is feeding me, spooning a soft-boiled egg from its shell, as well as the pulp of a big ripe tomato. And, as I open my mouth to receive the spoon, my mother's lips move with mine. To this day I remember how soothing the blend of egg and tomato felt in my mouth, and, again, I look at my mother with love and infinite gratitude. Children are so earnest in their emotions, their little hearts fill up with love."

"So true."

"And my mother, too, as she feeds me, has this gentle, soft look in her blue eyes. She had the most beautiful blue eyes."

"The world is cruel to gentle souls," Sabine says quietly, and Nadja nods. "My mother never fed me," Sabine adds.

"I'm sure she did, she must have. You just don't remember it."

"Maybe." Sabine thinks a moment, then picks up the menu. "What about dessert?"

"Let's share one. You order, you're good with desserts."

Outside the restaurant, just before they part, Sabine has an idea. "Why don't you come out again before I close La Casa for the winter? Come for a week or two and bring your computer. You can work on your novel, and I promise to leave you alone. No distractions."

"Are you sure?" The image of the two of them working in the same house but in separate rooms appeals to Nadja.

"Positive. And it will help me to have you around while I work on my own stuff. So you'll be doing me a favor."

"Hmmm." Nadja is still weighing the pros and cons. She is thinking out loud. "What about Raoul?"

"Raoul can wait," Sabine says, helping Nadja to decide and say that yes, she will come and spend a week or two at La Casa.

They are having an Indian summer and everyone, it seems, is out on the street, enjoying this unexpected gift of clement weather, something they all so richly deserve. Life in the city is hard, so a bonus is deeply deserved and deeply appreciated. On the whole, Nadja is having a blessed day, strangers on the street smile at her, and it's easy for her to believe that everything is working in her favor. She has adjusted to her not-so-new situation and feels secure in it. And she and Raoul have agreed to not be lovers anymore, but to try and remain friends, meeting once or twice a month in a restaurant to talk and catch up. Her novel is advancing well, even if Woman is not in very good shape. Such blessed days, Nadja knows, do not last long, but she is determined to enjoy this one for as long as she can. And tomorrow she will be leaving the city for two weeks to stay with Sabine and work. Vivian, with Sabine's permission, may join them for a day or two.

It is evening, and she is out on the street for a walk. She embraces her neighborhood and the multitude of ethnicities in casual wear: no suits, no ties, no important airs. Humanity in clusters of spiked hair, lean bodies, spurs. Haphazard collections of salable goods spread out on the pavement on blankets: a pair of crumpled shoes, old magazines, a couple of paperbacks. She has read somewhere that in Russia the poor buy from the poor—an old pot, a hat—but here she has yet to see someone stop and examine the goods, let alone make a purchase. It appeals to her, though, the idea that she, too, could clean out her apartment of old things, try to sell them on the street and so engage in the entrepreneurial spirit of the city. As kids, she and her friends sold lemonade during the summer. Indoors, on rainy days, they liked to pretend they owned a drugstore with a ringing cash register. Once, the register did not stop ringing; they made a fortune that day.

In the crowd, a tall man stands out, feeding a muffin to his baby daughter, perched on his chest in a sling. He stops for a moment, intent on his daughter as she pushes her mouth into the muffin and nibbles on it, and it is clear that, just then, nothing exists for him but the baby he is holding, her mouth, the muffin. Nadja is always moved when she sees a male so attentive and tender with a child. It is as if she needs occasional reminders that males, too, are part of the human race.

She stops to gaze at posters in the window of a travel agency. She could buy a one-way ticket and fly to a small fishing village in Greece where the living is cheap and one's needs are minimal. She may decide to stay there, live out her days by the sea, a foreign recluse among the locals, a topic of curiosity, gossip, perhaps pity, or worse, derision. She may become an eccentric, like the old, disgruntled lady she noticed the other day in the park, barking at a hopeful squirrel: "Nothing for you, buddy."

Teenage boys go past her, and one of them says in a loud, peacock voice, meant for her ears, "Give me an older woman any day. I want a woman to teach me something for a change." She is tempted to put him in his place and shout something back, like, "Older women don't like cocky boys," but of course she refrains, accepting that in the eyes of teenagers she is ancient. She takes revenge in the thought that some day, possibly sooner than he imagines, this boy will seem ancient to others. Last year, she was dancing in a club with Deirdre when suddenly, out of nowhere, two boys, eighteen or nineteen, swiftly moved in on them, one appropriating Deirdre, and the other Nadja, effectively separating them and taking charge. Nadja admired their spunk and verve, their well-orchestrated offensive and, for a moment, flattered by the attention, she toyed with the idea that since she and Deirdre do sport a youthful look, maybe they could, at least for a while, flirt with the boys. But soon the boys realized their mistake and, just as swiftly and suddenly, they vanished, off to conquer other turf.

A man, carrying a suitcase, is suddenly at her side, startling her. "Excuse me," he says. "Can you tell me what a nightingale is?"

Nadja tries to remember if there is a bar or a restaurant in the neighborhood named The Nightingale, surmising that this is what the guy is looking for. He has a trace of an accent, maybe European.

Nothing comes to mind, but before Nadja has a chance to respond, the man says, "It's a bird, isn't it?"

Nadja looks at him, at his suitcase tied with a rope, and is now alert in a different way. "Yes," she says slowly, "it's a bird."

"I thought so," the man says and walks on.

So much frailty and confusion in one city, Nadja reflects. She actually appreciates this sort of benign confusion which, on certain days, touches them all.

Later, around eleven o'clock, she is out on the street again, this time for a quick walk around the block, and on the lookout for a cigarette butt. She has had a full, good day of work and she's entitled to a little shnickle, packed with comfort. Up the block, she notices an old woman stooped over a profusion of small flowers around a tree in front of an apartment building;

as she approaches, Nadja realizes that the woman is pruning the flowers. Nadja is enchanted: she has been going past this building for years and never noticed the flowers before. "These are beautiful flowers," she says, and the woman looks up at her, smiles and says, Thank you, and Nadja resolves to always notice the flowers when she goes past.

She continues on her way, feeling buoyant, free. There is a light breeze, there are people all around her, talking, laughing. The night invites a variety of characters to come out and she congratulates herself for being among them, all the while scanning the sidewalk for a good-looking butt. She does not need much, just a couple of puffs, to go nicely with a sip of wine, and so conclude the day. She does not like the thought that she robs the homeless, but she has a ready excuse: she is trying to save money and also to quit smoking and therefore does not buy cigarettes anymore.

Here, she spots her prize. Looking around her, making sure no one is watching, she picks up the butt. She checks the brand: a Camel—many Camel smokers in her area. She rubs the filter between her fingers to clean away any lingering germs, and walks home.

Upstairs, she smokes the precious butt by the open window, and then goes into the bedroom. The days ahead will bring more of the same, but it is a "more" she can tolerate: more jogging, more reading, more of Woman Ending Badly. For Woman, summer has just begun, but outside Nadja's window, winter will soon arrive.

Nadja climbs onto the bed and props up the pillows. She feels a little old doing this, maybe lonely, aware as she is of every movement she makes. It is strange that she should feel this way, and yet, it is a moment that invites introspection as she goes through the motions, preparing for sleep. She pulls up the covers and reaches for Lagerkvist's *The Dwarf*. She reads: "I have noticed that sometimes I frighten people; what they really fear is themselves. They think it is I who scare them, but it is the dwarf within them, the ape-faced manlike being who sticks up its head from the depths of their souls. They are afraid because they do not know that they have another being inside them. They are scared when anything rises to the surface, from their inside, out of some of the cesspools in their souls, something which they do not recognize and which is not a part of their real life. When nothing is visible above the surface, they are utterly fearless. They go about, tall and unconcerned, with their smooth faces which express nothing at all. But inside them is always something else which they ignore and, without knowing it, they are constantly living many kinds of lives. They are so strangely secretive and incoherent."

Her eyes beg sleep, and Nadja struggles to keep them open. There is a certain reluctance to let go of the day, to place the marker in the book and call it a night.

ABOUT TSIPI KELLER

Tsipi Keller was born in Prague, raised in Israel, studied in Paris, and now lives in the U.S. A fiction writer and a translator of Hebrew literature into English, she is the author of twelve books, and her short stories and novel excerpts have appeared in journals and anthologies in the U.S. and abroad (in German, Romanian, and Hebrew translations. She is the recipient of several literary awards, including the National Endowment for the Arts Translation Fellowships and New York Foundation for the Arts Fiction grants.